THE SHIFT

Augustin Cambau

HYPERIDEAN PRESS

Hyperidean Press C.I.C.
www.hyperideanpress.com

Edited by Udith Dematagoda and Lydia Sviatoslavsky

The Shift – First Edition April 2024

Cover: *Dead in the Grass* by Augustin Cambau © 2023

ISBN 978-1-9163767-7-9

Well! This was no small breakthrough! I suddenly desired to urinate.
And again, watching my urine stream out, everything stopped.

—The Autobiography and Maxims of Master Han Shan

He lay on a bench,
confused and unwell
but a silent thing came
and changed him.

He laid himself down on the bench, after a while, because he was unable to stay upright. He hasn't done anything all day, has simply let himself drift from corner to corner of this central square of a small town in the Caribbean (they call this square Zocalo), from bench to bench, under the variegated shapes of tropical trees, sometimes listening to the birds, sometimes watching people pass by, especially the women; and feeling guilty because of this, he starts to also look at the men, at their legs and their bellies, and imagines touching their hairy skin, smelling it. He has decided that he somehow has a duty to be symmetrical, and so he fantasizes more about men to compensate his reflexive, inelegant and acute awareness of feminine bodies passing by. This is what his thoughts are doing. He changes positions on the bench, holding himself up on the left then the right elbow, then the left one again.

Sometimes, though - not all the time but when he remembers to - sometimes, he holds his breath in, creating holes in the constant and dizzying flow of his thoughts. Holes! Chasms, columns of refreshing vapour, ancient gilded sceptres, gems of untold purity, and catching all the light... Holes, delightful emptiness, a fragile thing, and that last only moments. It only works when he holds his breath in, and to do that intently he would need more strength than he has at his disposal, so there's no way to truly pursue it. His is a crooked state, though the holes do make it better; in his mind, the holes are what he is doing with his time today. That and interesting explorations around his projected sexuality. From this account, to himself and for himself, of what he is doing with his time, he could exclude, or indeed is excluding, the pervading feeling of dirtiness, of being soiled, that accompanies his every thought and movement and intention. Except for the holes.

He has sat his body up again, weakly, when something happens. Something wholly undeserved, and it takes him - a resolution to the buzzing of his mind. It is resolved. His unclean state has allowed all the dregs to rise up to the surface (a tiring state of affairs) but then his tiredness just sort of opens up and --- now, a new sensation exists inside of him. Maybe this is sloth still, but in that case it is divine sloth, because it truly is delicious. Like when they give you morphine when you're in pain, at the hospital. The transition is similar; the result is probably better, but there is no way to know. Obviously this should be surprising, as sudden shifts like this one are not common; but there actually isn't space for a feeling like surprise within this new state. Everything that was there inside before is still there, but now all these things, instead of being jagged-edged and irksome, are contained somehow, and glowing, humming; gently tickling mind-objects they are now. Now he is satisfied, like a cat. He's foggy inside, and soiled by his unrestrained and babbling mind, but at the same time, he isn't soiled, he is untouched, is different from it : it doesn't matter as much. In fact, it just doesn't matter at all.

Has someone drugged him in a way he doesn't know of? Possibly. There are stories about a terrifying drug from Colombia that you simply need to smell to become a compliant docile being, susceptible to accept anything anyone asks you to do. The idea amuses him. It really doesn't matter to him; not on the left, not on the right, not on top of him or underneath- it doesn't matter anywhere. It wouldn't matter if he were horny, or happy because of some flattery, or thinking of death, or was speaking on the phone, or was being pestered by an acquaintance for money, or something, anything else. In any and all of these states, in any direction they may occur or arrive from, it doesn't matter, doesn't matter, doesn't matter - truly it doesn't. It's all equal. It's pleasant and also unpleasant, and so it is nothing that should preoccupy him.

And underneath this new feeling, this vapour, there's also something like a prickle; like a thorn: an unbearable sensation, as though it were pulling at him from the inside, that indicates to him that he is just

truly just on the brink of,

right there,

almost there, on the edge,

here

on the other side of, but just barely

behind a thin wall or membrane or veil, the thinnest thing

just on the brink of the resolution of all this. All of This. The answer. The microfilm with the plan (or something) where It is all laid out, precisely, organically, perfectly; whereby all mysteries and questions are rendered obsolete, and with them all the questioning, the empirical research, the fail and fail better, all the things which are mixed and composite; every mixing of things, every single definition, and probably all intellectual discursive activity. It is right there. But just behind. He isn't quite there. Almost, but not quite. It's almost painful, it could almost rip his heart out, but only almost. It's simultaneously just fine and dandy, absolutely terrifying, and not at all important; doesn't matter. His heartbeat is slow but powerful.

He has lain himself down on the bench, with one elbow resting between two of the band of metal the bench is made of, and outwardly nothing has changed, except a sigh he lets out, which is a sigh of relief. He has let it out as if to test this new state of things, of which he hopes it'll stay. And inside, there's this kind of vapour that makes everything equal.

AIRPORT

The airport hall is wide and white, and most of the surfaces are pretty smooth, and the sounds are typical muffled airport sounds, and the people are typical airport people. Some run, some walk, some sit and some lie down, reclining on their luggage next to phone chargers, and looking at their phones, or sleeping on the floor. One of the rare places you'll see non-marginal people sleeping on the floor, he thinks, and then doesn't think any more. He's just taking it all in. Every single movement he makes is perfect, as though his mind were clear and organised and perfectly present in the moment, even though there are rockets and fireworks going off inside his ribcage. He is elated. He doesn't want or need a cup of coffee, a sandwich, or to go on the internet. He gives away his suitcase in exchange for a boarding pass, goes through customs while smiling to everyone, and goes to sit where he's supposed to sit. It's a waiting room in an airport that resembles many other waiting rooms in airports. People wait, sleep, and look at their phones. He doesn't do anything; at one point he thinks he must look strange and out of place, sitting there, legs uncrossed, not doing anything, but it doesn't matter; there is something like a breath, a light wind, circulating between the aluminium seats, the tiled floor, and the people and their suitcases; if it were a real physical wind, it would ruffle his hair.

AIRPLANE

They told him to sit there, so he did. His neighbour seemed to envy his position by the window, so he offered to switch seats, which they did. He doesn't know why he did it. Normally, he wouldn't have. But in that case, isn't he in a normal state? He patiently, calmly, examines all the mistakes he might be doing, or things he might be forgetting, in thinking that everything is pretty much OK. None convinces him. He sits there for eight hours straight, with a stable, relaxed, slightly smiley look on his face. His forehead is exceptionally smooth and unwrinkled. Thoughts come by and pass, and kindly he watches them pass by, listens to them, and sees them leaving through the corner of his eye. After eight hours, he needs to piss, gets up, asks the attendant if he can go, she says yes, he pees, washes his hands, and comes back out. When he sits back down, part of his mind is trying to remember whether he looked at his reflection in the mirror or not. He remembers the attendant's face. A puff of information, something akin to a memory, takes possession of him as he recalls the lock of blonde (dyed) hair that stuck out of her attendant's hat.

Three or four hours later, the plane is flying over France, (which he knows because there's a little map on the screen in front of him where a small red airplane indicates the position and direction of the actual airplane), then, moments later, above Paris it starts manoeuvring. How tiny France is, compared to the ocean! It isn't all that stupid to notice that. But it isn't all that interesting, either. He has an erection when it is time to get up and leave the plane. On the inside, it makes him laugh; on the outside, he holds his bag in front of his crotch.

PARIS

Luggage, customs, do you wish to declare anything, he doesn't, it is night, it is cold. Everyone around is rushing about and seems preoccupied. He helps a lady, who is alone with two kids, to carry her bag. She thanks him a lot. He really doesn't know how to react to all that, so he doesn't. He's not sure whether he's actually present with her; his helping hand was meaningless to him. Outside, he wonders whether Valentine actually has or hasn't said that she'd come pick him up in the car. He thinks she has. Anyway, he's smoking a cigarette. Valentine arrives, as a group of angry people pass by, annoyed at a suburban train strike. He'd just finished making a face at them, a kind of understanding but blasé scrunching of the features, when he noticed Valentine.

She's smiling widely and her hair is very elegantly done. She's wearing an exquisitely cut black coat, and red lipstick. He feels proud to know and frequent such an elegant person. She hugs him, kisses him joyfully, seems happy and smells very good. It's true, he remembers, that things weren't all that great when he left Paris; she was supposed to come, and didn't. But he did, and spent two weeks away from her in the Caribbean, and now they're together again. The skin under her eyes is a little dark beneath her delicate make-up, but truly she seems happy. Looking more closely, he can detect something lingering around her pale blue eyes, like a viscous liquid. But he's happy to see her, and that she smells so good; she's happy too; her smiles are joyous and frank . They walk to the car (she carries one of his bags) while talking about airplanes and travels in a general way. Later, on the motorway, as she's concentrating on her driving (she's very pretty when she's concentrating), she half turns towards him, concentrates on the road again, and then starts telling him the important things she'd undoubtedly thought of telling him, as she prepared to come pick him up: she doesn't reproach him with anything. She has forgiven him for leaving without her. She understands. On her side, it hasn't been easy to face all of it, the funeral, her whole family crying, the concerned friends, etc. without him; especially day-to-day, where she would've needed his steady, supportive presence. She's been impatiently waiting for him.

She needs him, she says. He looks at her, curiously and with a smile, and places a lock of her pale hair behind her ear, gently brushing her diaphanous temple, white and delicate, where a blue vein is clearly seen. It was something like what had occurred to him fleetingly, when he was thinking of the lock of blonde (but dyed) hair of the flight attendant, dangling from her flight attendant's hat. He tells her that he's here now. He tells her that when he was over there, he wasn't truly over there, he doesn't remember having done or seen anything. Or one thing: there was a lot of water everywhere. He doesn't know why he had to go, even without her. But now he's here. He thanks her for forgiving him, sincerely, though he isn't ashamed of having left. He isn't sure, as he's saying all this, whether his statements are truthful or not, but at the same time no refutation to his own claims arises within him. Maybe he could be a little more precise, but he's unable, right now, to articulate things any more than this.

For a split second, she half opens her mouth, as though surprised by what he's saying and about to object to it; but she closes her mouth again and smiles, and then it's her turn to extend her right arm toward him, and she touches his hair. They have touched each other's hair; everything is alright. There is palpably more to say about all this than what has been said, but the priority here is obviously to witness and manifest the love and tenderness that is between them; for now this is what is needed. The car exits the ring road, and enters Paris.

IT ALL CONTINUES

He left because the trip was already booked and paid for, he didn't really know the uncle, and he needed a holiday. She stayed because of duty. Outwardly they agreed that it made sense for him to go and for her to stay; but on the inside this turn of events has made him a deserter, and made her deserted; which is something they both feel the other is open to figuring out. But not right now. The foundation for this moment is the bond between them, and this bond exists before and beneath all the conversations that they might have about it. That is the precious thing here; hence how precious their silence is.

Having parked the car in its parking space, they go up to the apartment (again, she carries one of his bags), and then they sit on the couch and speak and touch each other's arms and face, and thighs, and soon thereafter they take off all of their clothes, not very fast, as we do when desire can't be contained, but not slowly either, as when everything is sacred and slow and we are hyper-conscious of every movement and its perfection within the flow of things. They each help the other to undress, kissing all the while, taking their time and not making a show of it, with the manner and rhythm that best corresponds to this situation, where there are definitely things in the background, like when some mud is mixed in with the water and floats there, slowly falling back down; and at the same time it is quite certain that they are a pair, the unity of two beings, as much as they know how to be that. They make love on the couch, and then briefly on the floor, and then on the kitchen counter, and they stop at one point to have a glass of water and eat the remainder of a chocolate cake (it's delicious), and they go to the room presumably to sleep, as symbolically unity has been achieved and they now deserve some rest, but they have more sex there, for a long time, quite entranced, not speaking much. Every movement is intended as proof, for the other, and verification, for one's self, that they are truly willing to give this now: their body, their trust, their forgiveness, especially their bodies right now, but also the other things, and sincerely. This is alternated with moments of devilish joy, wide eyes, liquids everywhere, teeth, tongues, pumping, grins, brutality almost, a type of feeling he had forgotten could be had while he was away, but that he finds here again with elation. They both fall asleep after having exchanged some light words. He has come three times. Nothing really matters here, beyond staying within the flow of things, which demands no effort.

The following morning, she wakes up before him, as always, and leaves after having kissed him while he was in a fully lucid slumber. She has left a note where she says she loves him at the end, and in the middle asks him to take care of certain things. He gets up and goes to the kitchen to make coffee, automatically, naked in the kitchen, as always. In the background, he's thinking here we go, it's all starting again as before, continuing, but in the front it doesn't matter. He showers, before getting to work on all the things that, implicitly or explicitly, before others and his own self, he has previously decided to take on. What else would he do?

EVERYTHING JUST KEEPS ON CONTINUING

He has spent the whole day with his parents in the countryside, and now he's in the car, coming back. Valentine went to the pool with her best friends and the plan is to meet up to have dinner with friends. At one point during the afternoon, there was a lull (a hole, an ancient gilded sceptre, etc.) in the conversation, and he looked at his father's face and was again immersed in the pulsating sensation, unbearable, lingering, but packed in cotton wool and as such, bearable; this kind of pulling at, or prickling, by this sensation that isn't of the same nature as other sensations, because it bears with it the echo of other things (perhaps even all other things), exactly as though he was perceiving it from within a cave, as a sound accompanied by ultrasounds and infra-sounds- or something- and accompanied, furthermore, by other sensations, similar to sounds in nature but perceived by other, less obvious organs.

It's as though he had been running his fingers on a very thin skin and felt underneath a thin, elongated shape without being able to determine whether it was really there or not really there, and if it was, then that changes everything and did it have to be taken care of; should the skin be opened up with a scalpel? How to take care of it? Through what acts, what movements? What is the scalpel? It is almost intolerable, there is something like a victory cry stuck inside his chest; but also, really, it is a victory cry; truly I can leave it here. It doesn't bother me. I'd rather have a victory cry stuck beneath my throat than a cry of despair stuck in the cotton-wadded emptiness of my brain. Even though those two things are very similar, and perhaps even the same thing. And he keeps on driving, having at no point lost focus by this event that truly isn't that much of an event. And it's nice to be driving a modern car with all the soft lights on the dashboard, as the night is softly falling all around, and with a constant and very soft humming all around, as one is going to meet up with the woman one loves and friends, to have a drink and have dinner outside a restaurant. Some people suffer and have problems, but not him.

DRINKS WITH FRIENDS, TREASON

It's surprising to feel no limits to your energy. At one point, he remembers he would've suffered from having things to do, people to see, from not being in what he would've considered a good and pleasing situation. Now, it's all the same. He has been working all week with crazy stressed-out people, has endured it all and did everything he had to and more; he has spent Saturday doing things with Valentine that he didn't truly care for, because Valentine cared for them; in one sense, it was like helping the lady with her two children at the airport, even though Valentine wasn't thanking him, because in her mind he was doing all those things for himself, too. In life we are asked to do things, he thinks. Better to do them. Then he spent Sunday with his parents, whom he adores forever of course, but who can also get on his nerves with the eternal grinding of their habits.

He thinks all this, without really paying attention, as Valentine parks the car miraculously close to the bar they are going to. Some days are lucky days.

At the cafe terrace, their friends are all already there. It's a spring evening, everyone is Parisian and nonchalant, having a nice Parisian moment in the warm night air, with sweet smells of food, perfume and tobacco smoke wafting about. Did someone walk behind him in the street, walking fast and bearing an anguished and sad look, like a ghost? He didn't really see. It makes him think of terrorist attacks that have happened before at café terraces like this one. Part of him imagines the shift a terrorist attack would effect upon this tranquil spring atmosphere, where everybody is lounging around. All other parts of him are simply walking toward the table where their friends are, smiling slightly. Not one part answers the part that was imagining a terrorist attack. Not one is considering trauma, collective trauma, the scale of collective trauma from benign (his case) to extremely heavy, as is the case of some people he has met, who have suddenly found themselves with a dying spouse between their arms without ever expecting such a thing could happen. Not one. The conversation doesn't happen.

They sit down with their friends, not next to each other. He sits between a girl he has known for a long time and whose body he has coveted for a time, though that isn't so much the case recently, and a boy who is a satellite of the group, but about whom no one seems to know much. Valentine has sat next to the girl who is her favourite friend at this table, between this girl and another boy, who has smiled in a worldly way as they arrived, and produced some traditional jokes to greet them. If this boy had been a part of our parents' generation, he would wear his hair slicked back and a signet ring. It is thought that this boy enjoys football.

The conversation follows the usual scheme. News about one another's lives are given, one remembers this or that thing about another's life, asks a question about it, and it bounces around in this way, with digressions about subjects that appear in the course of conversation; sometimes everyone is concentrating on the same conversation, and sometimes the table is divided in several sub-conversations, intimate and whispered, or superficial and humorous, and in louder voices. Sometimes someone makes a joke and everyone laughs, and sometimes someone is outside the conversation for a while, fidgeting with something or observing something or doing something on their phones. At one point, Valentine even stands up to speak on the phone, and the friend who would wear his hair slicked back if he were a part of our parents' generation turns his head toward her, and looks at her curiously, as though he were truly wondering who she might be talking to, and about what, as though he had in his possession the elements that would allow for such speculation.

He acquires in this exact moment the absolute and undeniable knowledge that this boy and Valentine have had sex together. His reaction is one of slight surprise, even curiosity. When Valentine comes back, she deliberately averts her eyes from the boy, and the boy, on the other hand, watches her with a certain intensity, an intensity that he disguises as indifference. He immediately acquires the utter and certain knowledge that they have only had sex together once or twice, and that she ended the relationship quite recently, and that he would like for it to start again, or at least to remind Valentine of the fact that they have had sex together. It is absolutely clear. He isn't offended, he doesn't even have to pretend not to be offended. He has acquired information, and it echoes in him rather like the memory of scream, a scream in the dark, a scream intent on being found, to have its case examined; it is an old scream, not a current one; either a memory, or a prediction. There are also hidden flashes of erotic imagery, skin on skin, open lips, erect penis, Valentine holding it in herself, etc. But they are like a test, a series of tests; they provoke no reaction other than the echo of that scream. An echo in a cave.

After having observed Valentine, the boy turns toward him, a reflex action designed to ascertain his ignorance of what has transpired, and then he quickly covers up the reflex with a pretty mediocre joke. He laughs exactly as he would have laughed if he hadn't acquired the information he has just acquired: politely. And then he goes back to his conversation with his neighbour, the girl, after having looked compassionately in Valentine's direction, certain that she must be feeling uneasy, a prey to shame and remorse, as he knows her. The aim of his look in her direction was to reassure her. She seemed surprised. He doesn't know where such a detached and philosophical attitude could possibly be coming from, but since it's here, he isn't unhappy about it.

He speaks with his neighbour (who knows her history of art) about Bauhaus, and the marvellous ambitions that lived in those people. She agrees and expresses her admiration for the physical, palpable objects that came out of these ambitions, that, according to her, indicate that they were arriving, at that moment, at some kind of collective truth, in a "proof in the pudding" sort of way. He agrees, and is unable to try expressing (and even less to actually express) an idea that comes to him, that this truth seems in a way to have eluded them, not to have belonged to them. The conversation then becomes general again. It is a sweet and perfumed evening, the food they have ordered arrives. No terrorist attack on the horizon.

THEY GO BACK HOME

Even so, since acquiring the utterly undeniable knowledge that this boy and Valentine have had sex together, something lingers on his mind. Why is he so unaffected? This is very unlike him. He would've expected to react with despair, something like a chasm opening inside him, a chasm in which he would have fallen, out of control, also with anger, maybe even hatred, perhaps even a longing for physical violence, etcetera etc. But no. He has looked at Valentine with an entirely and sincerely compassionate intention. And now they're in the car (he's driving now), and still nothing dramatic has happened within him. Does he not love her anymore? He looks at her and feels love; so that can't be it.

Valentine, on the other hand, is silent and nibbling at her nail. She knows he knows. She, too, has acquired a certainty: she has no choice, she must now face this unpleasant situation. He thinks he knows that the infidelity can't be an entirely meaningless thing for him, because Valentine is known for her commitment to monogamy. She subordinates the importance of pleasure and exploration and fun for purposes of knowledge and self-exploration to many other, more old-fashioned things, as a part both of her received education and her character. She might be able, though, to convince herself that she's acting upon the desire for such things, he thinks, because people do that, and also it would be more complicated to face the actual causes of the impulse, causes he knows nothing about (maybe their outline is appearing imprecisely in his mind), and she knows nothing about either, all the while knowing them intimately, of course.

In any case she's about to speak. She's preparing her defence, reflexively. It is what is done in these situations, even though maybe, at the same time, she is taken over by a comforting cloudy feeling of resolution, of a knot being untied. Maybe something in all this is weighing on her, perhaps the discrepancy between his own attitude and what Valentine expects from a companion; maybe that's what she was expressing, for herself and for the world, by sleeping with this boy who, it is thought, likes football.

The idea comes to him (as a good joke comes to a person, but with the sensation of a stream of vapour against his ribcage, from the inside, that could almost make him vomit), that maybe she resents him for his detached and philosophical reaction to the discovery. Maybe some part of her hoped that a fit of jealousy would do her work for her.

But, nothing. The nail-nibbling goes on until they get to the apartment (the silence is heavy during this interval). Finally, he's the one to ask whether she has something to say, because he can see she's obviously ruminating over something. It is a passive way of taking matters into his own hands, but it works; she looks him in the eye for the first time in a while, as though she were surprised and shocked; it seems like for a second she had tried to act as though everything were normal and he was being paranoid. But he is looking at her with a sweet and tender gaze.

Once again, he is feeling that he is just on the brink of something enormous, something final and definitive; and maybe this huge something is conflated in this very moment with whatever it is she is about to say, because her words indeed have the potential to change a few things, seemingly important things, but at the same time he has to know that this is mostly about something else. And Valentine doesn't speak, and becomes withdrawn again, but now she knows that her time is up, she can no longer stay silent and prepare her defence. She must speak, because she has admitted through her movements that she has something to say. And she speaks.

She says it was nothing, truly he needs to understand this, that she was feeling very lonely and powerless before the death of her dear great uncle and all the family turmoil that had surrounded his death, that she had needed him, but he wasn't there, and she had done it out of a form of spite and because the situation had presented itself, but it was only once.

He knows he should defend himself. This is how the situation should unfold. He should come up with a nasty, brutal retort (it should come irrepressibly from his gut), that would then provoke a lively discussion, perhaps even an argument where both would scream, and the argument would finish well or badly, according to what is possible for them in that moment. What is required is a scene whereby the traditional structural scheme is followed, introduction-augmentation-apex-resolution; it is what is demanded by all of their experiences of the world, and all the love songs they've ever listened to.

But, instead of retorting, he does not retort. He looks at her big blue eyes, where he can almost see tears; big, viscous tears. And he keeps looking. I think he's trying to come up with something certain, something upon which he might lean on to express something to her. He is still feeling, in his belly, that the truth is very close, but the sensation is progressively losing in intensity as he concentrates on the eyes of Valentine. The way he's looking must be rather strange to her; interrogating, curious, concentrated on a problem that must be solved, but not very intense- it is a soft way of looking. The truth of him, at this time, is that he doesn't know what to say, because he doesn't know what he wants, because he can't be sure that he actually wants something. Or maybe he does, but only one thing: he wants her not to be sad, not to be holding back thick, painful tears. And because he has no idea how to obtain this thing he wants, he does the only thing that he's capable of at this time: he tells the truth. Or in any case his own version of it. He tells Valentine, as he looks inside her eyes that are blue and sad, that he's not sure what to make of all this, that he's really sorry, but he doesn't feel sad, or cheated, or jealous, or anything, he just wants her to feel better and to stop being sad. He tells her please trust me, tell me the truth, we'll see where that takes us. And then he hugs her, and she doesn't even hug back, but at last simply starts crying.

After some tears and even some small, salty kisses (because of the tears), they wind up sitting on the couch. Or rather, in the couch. What comes out is that she doesn't know, either, what it is that she wants. Of course, she wants to be normal, to be well, to be content; for this whirlwind to abate. But between this ideal state of affairs and the things she can conceive of doing today, a great chasm now exists. A hole. Not an ancient gilded sceptre type hole, either, but a scary one. How complicated life is! He has no solution to offer; but he finds himself telling her something he hasn't said before, but that has been on his mind for a while: he wouldn't mind leaving Paris, this life they are leading of being active, fashionable almost-thirty-year-olds doesn't suit him. He would like to live with more plants than humans around him. He says he's been offered a job, a job he could work at from anywhere, for one year, and renewable, and that would pay decently; he has been contemplating renting a house somewhere down south, and getting away from Paris a little bit.

In the serious, vast and empty atmosphere that they have now settled inside of, that which feels like the aftermath of a storm, he starts to gently talk about this plan, a plan that he hadn't seriously considered until now. She listens, sometimes sniffling a little bit.

It is now as though a candle had been lit and put there, in front of them, on the white lacquered table, and its small yellow flame were reflected in their eyes. As though he had provoked the existence of a magical lamp, and the lamp was projecting a thousand small lights all around the floor and walls and ceiling of the living room, that opens on the kitchen, and on top of the taupe coloured rug, and on the mantelpiece of what used to be the chimney, made of old porous stone, now a solely decorative object, that they are facing; they are children again, or dreamy adolescents, snuggled up in her sober and elegant Roche-Bobois couch; they dream of the south.

It is possible materially, financially; they make sure of that quickly- so it is, indeed, possible. They light up, speak of lavender and cicadas- they even speak of cows, before remembering that cows aren't the most likely animal deep down in the south of France, a landscape they are now reconstructing from an array of motley elements, memories and things seen in films and also dreams. They aren't really making plans, but at the same time they are; they are adults, who put their dreams through tests and trials and calculations of feasibility, and the result of that is also, at this time, miraculously positive.

A hope is born in her; he's enjoying the atmosphere. They keep talking, and breathing life into this idea of going south (What would she do? She would write, and she would pick tomatoes and basil and rosemary to make salads), more and more, and then they fall asleep where they are, on the couch, in the flickering lights of their magical lamp, without showering or brushing teeth, or programming an alarm for the morning, or any of the things that a responsible person does.

THE FOLLOWING DAY

He wakes up alone, as always. Even without an alarm set, she must've woken up out of sheer habit. He's still in the sofa, but lying down now. Not a trace of Valentine, who must've left for work. He gets up and goes to shower. In the shower, as the water wakes him, two things become clear: first, he is happy, because he may have doubted the resiliency of his equanimous ghost yesterday, and maybe he has told himself that everything would fall apart and become as before after a hideous scene. But it hasn't. Second, on top of (or around) the happiness; he can feel that all of this matters not very much, including his joy - which renders his joy so authentically joyful. This isn't the type of joy that depends on external objects in order to exist. It seems to have to do with Valentine and with the south, but he knows that it's not deeply the case. He now thinks of Valentine's cheating only fleetingly (it appears, more and more, to not be very important), and of the man who would wear a signet ring and his hair slicked back if, etc....nor does he reflect very deeply about the relief he has guessed in Valentine, when he felt that she maybe wished to be liberated of him, of them, by a true crisis.

He doesn't reflect upon what he's supposed to do, either. He gets out of the shower, dries himself with a sweet smelling towel, doesn't forget to conscientiously brush his teeth (in small circles, as the dentist taught him), and gets out of the bathroom, naked, slowly, and goes toward the kitchen. It is surprising just how much his head isn't aching.

In the kitchen, he pours himself some coffee and opens his computer before him on the counter, as always. And, without thinking about it particularly, certainly not thinking that he's doing something very momentous, he accepts the job offer that he hadn't truly thought about till then, that will allow them to go live down south. She will be happy, and he will stay neutral, he thinks. And, at the same time, happy. Or at least, the part of him that is all draped up in a ghost that makes everything equal, important and unimportant at the same time, that is to say, the part of him that isn't the ghost, that part is happy to know that he will be happy and she will be, too. All around that, the ghost is still there. He is starting to rather like it, but doesn't dare think of it (of them?), because it might be changed by conceptualizing it.

He hasn't thought till then that it may be a ghost, and truly he still doesn't think that. He hasn't felt compelled to name or describe it, or them, so far; it hasn't felt special enough perhaps.

Now, after having accepted the job offer, he remembers a character in his childhood school books that was a kind ghost and appeared to help explain simple grammatical and mathematical ideas to the children using the book;

it was called Gaffi the ghost. Secretly, he says something like thank you, Gaffi, or hi Gaffi, it's nice, this, we aren't giving a fuck, not a single one of them, no idea what you're doing here but happy to know you, truly. And, at the same time, he feels a kind of flickering or vacillation in his torso, a flash of the impression that he is just on the brink of; and then suddenly, something like the beginning stages of a feeling, a true feeling, not the type of feeling that is all wrapped up in the robes of a benevolent ghost. He hardly has the time to try it, this feeling, hardly gets a taste; it feels like fear, or love, or an extreme and unbreakable attachment to something in the apartment, their apartment, Valentine's and his apartment, something that is covering the white walls and the fuzzy taupe floor and the decorative mantelpiece and the Roche-Bobois sofa and the Ikea bookshelves. Something that participates in the very structure of the living room.

And then, the following moment, the fear or the love have gone, and the only thing left is the feeling that there is something inside the surface of all the parts that, together, form their living room, their kitchen, their apartment, at the very spot where the surface of all those parts meet the air, there is a texture, some kind of matter or energy of an unvarying type, whose texture is unique in the world and doesn't change, whether it covers a moulding on the ceiling, hairs on the rug, the television screen, or an armchair- it stays the same.

And the feeling has gone before having flowered, and the sensation still exists, but comfortably cradled in the folds of Gaffi's ghostly apparel. The texture exists, he can feel it quite clearly. But it doesn't matter. He now goes to the room to get dressed.

VALENTINE, ONCE MORE, ISN'T COMING

Valentine doesn't have very fleshy lips, but enough to be called sensual, and she paints them with red lipstick. Her hair is blonde (dirty blonde, as some say), and bobbed (but no bangs), very thin skin, white and diaphanous, with bones underneath that (one guesses) are delicate. Her eyes are blue and her wrists are thin. Her forehead is almost freckled, but not quite. It is slightly rounded, and gives off an impression of intelligence. She is intelligent. She is tough. The world is never aware when she's having a moment of weakness. She is refined and witty, active, independent, has an irreproachable sense of style, and doesn't lack common sense or even kindness. She is capable of giving everything when she loves and trusts someone. She doesn't have any shortcomings: she has characteristics, like everyone else. No one takes her off-guard. And Valentine has changed her mind. Her blue eyes have changed their mind. Her black eyelashes have changed their mind. She will not be moving her exquisite wardrobe; she's staying in Paris.

Those are the family of thoughts that are going through him as he walks along the platform, where a Very Fast Train is already waiting. He thinks he might spend the whole trip in the buffet car. He will stay there, without moving, for five hours; he will watch the night recede away as the sun rises, and then all of the cities and countryside, without doing anything else, without thought, without judgement. Within him are passing not exactly thoughts or feelings, but the shadows of the thoughts and feelings that he knows he is supposed to be thinking and feeling, that he should be letting pass through him. They pass (these shadows), and he watches.

They pass regularly, without conflicting with or undoing each other, without changing his step, or the noise of his suitcase rolling behind him, or the steady beating of his heart. Valentine is a girl who knows what she's doing, Valentine has pink and delicate nipples, Valentine was my wife and also my sister, Valentine stays in the Roche-Bobois sofa, stays in Paris, is keeping the apartment and the car; and I'm going down south, because, after all, why not? There seem to be as many reasons to go than not to go, and as many reasons to stay than not to stay. The trip has been set in motion, and for what reason, exactly, should he wish to interrupt the motion? Since all is equal. Valentine reproached him, said he was being hasty, and she didn't want to be separated again. She called him a coward. Is he a coward? Possibly. Is he walking toward a situation where he may find the possibility to confirm whether or not he is a coward? It doesn't matter much. She also told him that he had become weirder after his solitary trip to the Caribbean, and of course he can't deny that. He doesn't want to deny it, either; it isn't really on his mind.

TO COME OUT OF MONTPELLIER
SAINT ROCH TRAIN STATION

Now he is walking from the platform to the great
hall in Montpellier train station. No ghosts of thoughts
accompany the sound of his suitcase; and walking by his
side is his new friend Judith he met on the train because she
sat next to him and asked, in a way that was both impolite
and charming in its innocence, if they could switch seats so
that she may sit by the window. He said yes, and then they
talked. She told him about her life: she has a small house
with little bits of land scattered all around it, not far from
Montpellier, where she keeps a vegetable garden for herself,
and medicinal and aromatic herbs that she transforms into
oils, waters, macerations and tinctures that she then mostly
sells to a mysterious lab in the mountains somewhere. She
smiles often, and her demeanour is natural, but she also
seems like she could eat anyone or any object, life-form or
concept with her strong, white teeth. Her skin is tan and
her body is strong; it is a body that is noticeably present,
and she smells strongly of plants, and lightly of garlic. She
is fifty-something years old, but looks closer to forty. Her
health seems excellent. It shouldn't be the most salient
thing to focus on, but really he is impressed by her teeth.

For his part, he has told her of his plans to stay for
a few nights at an AirBnb in Montpellier, and then from
there to look for a little house in the countryside that he
might rent, to live and work in, a place to build fires and
watch plants grow. The innocence and lack of guilt with
which he expounded on his Parisian rootlessness amused
her, and she offered to put him up in her spare room (she

made sure there was no sexual ambiguity; she is obviously accustomed to being desired), and to stay there till he could find his small house in the countryside. He can stay for as long as he needs. He saw no objection, as she appears trustworthy and he is temporarily free from his fear of death- and so now, he is walking toward her car, by her side. She's a fast walker, and the wrist of the hand that's carrying her suitcase is wide and strong.

The hall in this train station is tall and luminous, mostly white and made of glass and metal. Very current, very sleek. Like being inside a huge futuristic whale. There are people everywhere, especially women, he feels. He feels neither good nor bad, but also is on the verge of ecstasy. It is much hotter here than in Paris, where the weather was mild. How easy it all is. He thinks that this lack of friction must be hiding a trap, not knowing whether he's joking to himself, or if his anxiety is genuine and founded.

feelings, but the shadows of the thoughts and feelings that he knows he is supposed to be thinking and feeling, that he should be letting pass through him. They pass (these shadows), and he watches.

IN JUDITH'S CAR

Judith has a pretty recent car which, in a way that is itself intriguing, surprised him. He was obviously expecting some old, noisy thing, full of character, maybe painted in a retro color like yellow, with a sellotaped mirror and adorned with trinkets, and with knives and shears and paintbrushes in an open glove box. But Judith's car is a fairly recent 4X4 that is clean both inside and outside, and the only peculiarity that reminds him of Judith is a pleasant smell of dried herbs. Night is falling, and they are driving on the motorway, passing through hills that are covered in thick green vegetation.

It is the countryside: the sky is wide and there is a horizon. The car glides along the recently built road among other cars that are also gliding, all together in the growing dusk. No one is speaking. There is no music. It is quite thrilling.

A MESSAGE FROM VALENTINE

Je comprends pas ce qui se passe en fait, ni pourquoi tu es parti…
Pourquoi tout doit être si bizarre avec toi? Normalement les gens se
quittent pour des raisons. J'espère que tu vas revenir bientôt. Je tiens
à toi. Je t'aime

I don't understand what is happening or why you
left… Why must must everything be so weird with you?
Normally, people leave one another for actual reasons. I
hope you'll come back soon. You're important to me. I
love you.

THE ANSWER

Franchement, moi non plus je ne comprends pas. Je t'aime moi aussi, mais je crois que j'avais besoin de quitter Paris. Apparemment toi tu veux rester. Peut-être que tu me rejoindras une fois que j'aurai trouvé une maison? Je tiens à toi aussi tu sais. Quand on a décidé de partir dans le sud, j'ai cru qu'on était tous les deux sincères. Je ne peux pas revenir en arrière. Je t'aime et tu me manques.

Frankly, I don't understand either. I love you, too, but I think I needed to leave Paris. Apparently, you want to stay. Maybe you'll join me later? You're important to me, too, you know. When we decided to move south, I thought we were both being sincere. I can't go back. I love you and miss you.

BLUE VELVET

Since this is a village, there are streets that are almost like corridors, between walls of mostly white, but also black, yellow and red stones, with windows from which are hung terracotta containers with earth in them and small flowers sticking out of the earth. He has been living here for a week and three days, and already feels quite accustomed to this plant-filled life, with the fresh and piercing light everywhere, and simple, delicious foods that make him swoon like a Parisian at a restaurant, which provokes derision from Judith.

He walks along this street, which to him, is more like a corridor than like a street, slowly, wearing espadrilles and with a big loaf of bread under his arm. This is it. He is arriving to where the windows of Judith's house are, and from where he is he can hear music coming from inside the house. It is a playlist he was listening to before going out for bread (there is a truck that brings bread to the village every morning); it is a playlist of songs by crooners from the fifties and sixties, and the song that is playing now is Blue Velvet, sung by Bobby Vinton, the same song that provoked the eponymous film by David Lynch. The rhythm is light, a little bouncy, like small hops or skips, regular and weightless, and the music is delicate, airy, very soft, very velvety, and quite blue.

He passes next to a plant that smells good (he thinks it's rosemary but maybe not). The sun is on his left arm but not on his back. A shiver of cold pleasure shakes his spine. He is almost giddy and almost stops; but he doesn't. He walks forward, opens the door that wasn't locked, what a luxury, and enters the freshness of the old stone walls, where the music is stronger, and the shiver returns. His body seems to have decided that he would be happy.

AN EVENT

Judith needed tools and wanted coffee, so she came back to the house around 2 PM this afternoon, in between two sequences of plant-related work. She drank her coffee on the massive wooden table in the living room, which opens onto the kitchen on one side. On the other side is a room where there is a piano and a desk, and where he spends most of his time working on his computer. The rooms are separated by wide arches of rough, pale stone.

He likes it when Judith is present; her being in a room is reassuring and a little bit sexy, like the way having sun on your skin is inherently sexy, or bathing in the sea. Presently he is not concentrating on his work, but wallowing in the feeling of liveliness he gets when Judith is in the room, though she may, as is the case at this time, only be accomplishing mundane activities like drinking coffee and reading a brochure. Sometimes she just drinks her coffee and does nothing else. He admires her old fashioned single-mindedness- she doesn't distract herself all the time.

When her coffee was half drunk, she turned towards him (he felt her turn toward him), and talked to him, not waiting for him to face her. She told him about two friends of hers who own a house not far from here. They are moving to the city, and they want to rent the house out to someone. She spoke about this as if it were an interesting thing in and of itself that she wished to share with him, but she was obviously mentioning it because she thought he might be interested in renting the place.

As he listens to her, there is inside of him the beginnings of a sadness, that of being unloved and rejected, and maybe he did something wrong that made Judith want to throw him out? The truth is, Judith's presence is like a large bonfire by the sea, scary somehow but also invigorating and warm, and the part of him that is like a domestic animal (like a dog) wants to stay close to her forever. Like a dog from a shipwreck might want to warm himself by a fire. But the rest of him understands almost entirely clearly that this was actually the plan from the start, and even though he's spent almost no time looking for a house to rent, the idea was that Judith would put him up in her house until he could find one for himself. The plan included the alluring idea of a house surrounded with soil and plants growing from it, where he could take a few steps outside the house every morning with a mug of coffee in his hand, looking around at the garden, and take care of the garden, and build fires. The plan also included Valentine, of course, but no matter. The image was alluring from Paris, and now it is both alluring and a little bit scary, because it has become more concrete, and it implies a way of life he has fantasized about, but now realizes he will need to learn. Still, how fantastically easy! The plan fulfills itself.

And so he tells Judith, as though incidentally, that he might be interested in renting the house, and he would like to meet the couple, and visit their house, and he loves staying here with her of course but that was the plan from the start, wasn't it?

She laughs a little with her strong teeth out and tells him that tomorrow, Thursday, there would be a small event in a small abandoned village not far from here, with a little choir that would sing Occitan songs, and the couple of her friends would be present at the event, and if he wanted, this was the perfect time to meet them. He hasn't been to a social event since his arrival, about fifteen days ago; besides he doesn't know anyone here apart from Judith and three old ladies from the village. The idea of a small concert in a small village with a little choir, with the notion of a potential house and a garden and fires now connected to it, is pleasing to him. So he answers, with an enthusiasm that he himself is surprised by that yes, he would go, he would love to go. Judith tells him they would go together, and then a few things about what she will do with the rest of her day today, and he answers with his own plans for the afternoon, and then they both smile (her jaw is wide and strong), and then she leaves. He goes back to work without another thought, like an automaton. Later on, his phone rings, and his spine tingles: another message from Valentine.

ANOTHER MESSAGE FROM VALENTINE

En fait tu veux vraiment me quitter. Je comprends de moins en moins. Si c'est à cause de ce qui s'est passé avec Arnaud, je comprends, mais tu m'as dit que tu me pardonnais, que c'était pas grave. Et d'accord, c'est pas toi qui m'as quitté mais moi qui ne suis pas venue, mais tu es parti un peu vite non? Tu trouves pas ça bizarre ? Qu'est-ce que ça veut dire tout ça?

So you're actually leaving me. I understand less and less... If it's because of what happened with Arnaud, I understand, but you told me that you'd forgiven me, and it didn't matter. And yeah, you didn't leave me: I was the one who didn't come, but you left pretty fast, didn't you? What does all this mean?

He decides to call her, and climbs up to the roof of the house.

THE LAKE IS BEAUTIFUL AT NIGHT
UNDER A FULL MOON

There is a lake in the centre center of this large valley, which is, in truth, a small valley- you can go through it in 20 minutes by car, but when compared to human bodies it's big, and the lake is the most remarkable thing one perceives, as a human, when standing in it. The lake occupies most of the surface in this large valley, and all around there are hills, hills that are higher and steeper and rockier on the right, and rounder and lower and leafier on the left, and on both of the other sides (the shorter ones), they are round and red when the sun shines, and round and black at night.

They are- himself, Judith, and the couple she told him about the previous day, and another man he knows very little about- on one of the shorter banks of the lake; and in this moment he is a few steps away from the group (they are having a conversation about mutual acquaintances), and he's observing the black surface of the lake, with the glimmer of the moon reflecting on it. He isn't really thinking that it's beautiful; in truth he's feeling that it is, and his thoughts are going from one element of the landscape to the next, round and round, maybe formulating their names in his head (beautiful hills, beautiful lake, beautiful vineyards, beautiful forest, beautiful lights of the village, beautiful moon, beautiful reflection of the moon, a bird), but without insisting, and with the unwavering conviction that this is, truly, quite beautiful. He's not thinking about his conversation with Valentine yesterday. He was sitting

on the roof, his back against the chimney, and looking at
the hill (Judith calls it "the volcano" because apparently
it once was that, long ago) that slopes up from where the
village is, all hazy looking pine trees and mean, prickly
bushes that look soft and comfortable from afar. They
both cried, not understanding the situation, but he cried
like a rock, like one block, and felt calm throughout and
afterward. There was confusion, but it didn't bother him so
much as make him sad. It bothered her, though, and as she
slapped her own head around with contradictory emotions
and ideas, and he nodded along, she grew more and more
frustrated at things. They hanged up with difficulty, but
without having come up with a new diagnosis or solution.
He had left Paris, not her, but now he was staying. She
had stayed in Paris, and hadn't followed him, not because
of him, but because she saw no real point in leaving. And
so she is over there, and he is here, by the lake, and he is
currently not thinking about her particularly.

The moon is very wide, pale and rotund, and high in
the sky; the light is blue and the trees are blue; there is a
subtle tension in the air, like a laugh, similar to when you
just had good sex and the body feels a bit electric, or like
before sex when sex is in the air and both parties know it,
without having discussed it necessarily, or, more precisely
but in a less explainable way, like before and after sex at
the same time. Tingles.

At one point, he gets the impression that someone is
walking behind him, someone sad and preoccupied, just
passing by with a heavy burden on their shoulders- but
also, at the same time, that's impossible, and there aren't

any terrorist attacks near a lake in department of Hérault, and then the impression passes and he forgets it; he watches the moon and he feels stupidly in love, in love in general. Valentine is just a part of it.

He now knows that he will probably live in Judith's friend's house; that, in any case, he would like that. The Occitan songs were rather funny in some cases, and in others, rather beautiful. There were men in the choir doing low men's voices, women doing clear women's voices, and some people doing voices in between the two. Wine was drunk, and meetings were had. He met the couple that who are Judith's friends, and found them to be very pretty and shiny, a shiny couple; to one of them, the house is his family's house that he now owns. They are moving to Montpellier for work-related reasons. They would like the house to be occupied by someone they like, it is important to them that this be more than a mere contract, that's what they explained to him, and he got on well with them. They like him. He's going to visit the house with them tomorrow, Friday.

The group meets up with him where he had stopped and sat down. They sit around him, silently, as though to respect his silence. He himself is feeling ripples coming from outside, from the moon and the lake, and also from the inside, from his body, it seems, that are stroking him a little bit, concurrently feeling like a vapour and like a bubbling of water.

There is a sort of tingling in the air, a jingling, like small bells, and also inside him, and he feels this sensation has the potential to take control of him and topple over everything that's in there. But that's not what it does. It exists both inside and outside a large block of cotton-wool clouds that occupy his torso and cranium. He feels stuffed by it, like a doughnut. There is, around the cranium region, something benign, that is saying "ok then, very well, it is beautiful, ha-ha-ha". When the others start talking again, he talks with them, slightly in the back seat, but not dissatisfied with his position. They are talking about things, symbols it seems, that he vaguely knows about but not in the way they are referring to them; as though they were something that was happening in the present. He participates, nonetheless, in the conversation, but he can tell that something isn't there in his own version of things that is there in theirs. He has the feeling of this being a special moment, a turn in all their lives, and wonders whether he's projecting this feeling on the others, or maybe this great beauty isn't a habitual great beauty for them either. In any case, everyone entirely agrees on one thing: the lake is very beautiful tonight, under the full moon.

A GARDEN AND SOME FIRES

They have been everywhere in the house, and they are now coming out into the garden. The house is large and old, the centre of what probably used to be some kind of agricultural or industrial land from pre-industrial times; it can house several families under its roof, and probably a few animals, too. There is a ground floor and a first floor, and downstairs a large kitchen with a fireplace, an equally large dining room with another fireplace, a large room that has been arranged into a workshop, with old rusty and greasy tools and nondescript metallic objects strewn about every surface; there are more rooms than he could count, and most have their own fireplace. The house is old, with thick walls, and gives off an impression of being from several periods simultaneously, because some parts have been modernised, whereas others look like they haven't changed since the forties or fifties. It is cool inside, much cooler than outside- the walls are thick, and all the floors are tiled. Red tiles, blue tiles, tiles with geometric motifs; it is a museum of tiles. From what he has seen as they walked around it, the house is a labyrinth, filled with objects and smells of all kinds, and full of books, comic books, clothes old and new, shelves, pictures, and plenty of faded bucolic paintings. The house is a very full one.

It sits in the middle of an enormous garden, if one can call it that, much bigger than what he imagined back in Paris, an image that was most probably based on his parents' garden in the suburbs. The garden has two natural barriers: the river on one side, and the road on the other. On the road side, the valley continues a bit and there is a long, narrow field, and then a short plateau with no construction at all. On the other side of the river, the hill abruptly rises, and is covered in trees. So there is more sky on the roadside, and less on the river one. When you stand in the field on the other side of the road, the taller hill (the riverside one) looks high and mighty, a great mess of bushy trees that ends in bare rock. The other hill, the roadside one, is only about as high as the house. This configuration isolates the house, insulates it, protects it from civilization, the men explain. There are natural walls around this, their paradise.

The couple want the tenant to take care of the garden, it's part of the deal. There is a vegetable patch, some fruit trees, a vineyard and a great diversity of medicinal and aromatic plants all over the place. Part of the garden near the house has been vaguely made into a living space, with a table, chairs, a hammock, and a place on the ground to build a fire and cook things with the embers. The ground hasn't been levelled or covered in concrete to indicate where civilization continues and then stops, as is it with his parents' house, where the outside terrace is a tiled surface, at ground level, ending with grass. Here, the ground is the ground: made of dirt.

As he's discovering all of this, and while the couple explain how the garden is organized, he remembers the last party he went to, in Paris, an eternity ago it seems-although it wasn't much more than a month ago. He drank immoderately, flirted verbally with several girls and boys, didn't dance (he doesn't dance) and left, in the last leg of the night, with a group of people he vaguely knew, in to an unknown apartment, where large quantities of cocaine were had till early in the afternoon the following day. It had been a good party: he was well-received, and let the events carry him on, drinking what he was given to drink, inhaling what he was given to inhale. His equanimous ghost, that night, had made the night sweet and relaxed, without hitches, without violence. He had gently floated through the events, congratulating himself on the personal luck that had given him access, for no good reason, to such worldly ease.

Now he is here, visiting this house and garden that are so clearly filled with stories, memories and beings that have nothing to do with himself or his experience of the world, and standing between the place that is for eating and relaxing, and the place that is full of plants, numerous and, in his opinion, all the same, even though the couple is explaining their diverse and specific uses, now, he thinks of that evening. And he doesn't experience a déjà-vu, because a party isn't a garden, but he has the feeling that the memory and the present moment go together well. He has that feeling, that's it.

And he asks questions about the plants, and jokes about hoping that the house has Wi-Fi, because he couldn't possibly remember everything they are saying, and they say, of course there's Wi-Fi, who do you think we are, plus you can call us if you ever have a question, and also we'd have to talk about it, but we would like to come back sometimes, during the weekends (not every weekend, don't worry), and we can keep showing you then. They are speaking in the future tense (and not in the conditional), about him living in the house, which is a good sign, because he's really enjoying the place. On the other hand he feels a bit out of place here, being the Parisian who hardly knows the difference between a tulip and a daisy, the uprooted man, well groomed and well dressed, who works from his computer, a man who truly has no idea what the fuck he's doing here, ever, and here he is, his immature and fleeting dream being realized point by point (apart from Valentine, of course), in a way that is, like his ghost, wholly undeserved. He feels this is, in a way, some kind of injustice. Part of him is identifying with an imaginary child, in the house, who would be in the house, of the house, in some real way, and who would see him, with his grey t-shirt that has a little blue pocket on the right side of the breast, him, in the garden, gazing at the plants without understanding a thing beyond his liking this, in general, and the child is saying, "who the fuck is this guy," but at the same time he has the flattering memory of the party, and the fact that all this is entirely legal, and after all, this is exactly how things are panning out, and at this point it's just easier to go along with it than to go against it, and of course the child doesn't even exist.

In spite of all these excellent reasons, and for the first time since the appearance of the ghost, he's feeling a little out of place, a little unwelcome, even though the couple is delightful to him and evidently think he would be the perfect tenant for the house, provided he finds an interest for plants, he'll learn, it's really quite simple, you'll see, it's the most natural thing in the world, and you get attached to them. By the time they get to the end of the garden, where there are tomatoes and squash and zucchini of various kinds, he has a kind of revelation: these two are as clean and groomed as himself, and they work on computers too. And the one who's from the north's shirt is grey. After this revelation, there are no doubts left. He wants to live here and learn about plants, and take a few steps outside the house with his coffee in the morning, as he looks out at the garden. He wants to go to other parties like the one by the lake the other day, and meet more people who are delicate and connected with nature, who consider being in a garden filled with plants a real activity, and speak of symbols as though they were real things that actually apply to current everyday life. He wants to go to markets and meet the people who sell things, and also the people who buy things. He feels that he might take root. None of all this, of course, is formulated with words- they are images, like flashes from films, that replace one another at great speed, and dissolve into one another, undercut by pleasant impressions, impressions of light, of heat, of earth, of vegetables, of smiles. The words that come to him are: "yes, I want this," three words he repeats mentally, then orally: "Yes, I want this. I'd like to live here, I mean. I love it here." They're loving this, too. A contract will be signed in three days. In the meantime, if he has any questions, etc. And then they offer a cup of coffee and he says yes, thinking they will drink it outside, in the garden, where there are chairs and a hammock. They drink it in the kitchen. No matter.

TAKING A FEW STEPS OUTSIDE THE HOUSE WITH YOUR COFFEE IN THE MORNING, WHILE LOOKING AROUND AT THE GARDEN

It is already warm out at 8 in the morning here, when you are in the sun and not in the shade. The coffee is made, he has a still-burning cup in his hand; the garden is high, there is no other way of saying it: the average height of the plants that aren't trees is about at chest height. It's very green; the trees are all in that colour (except the purple one), and the plants also. Except of course, there seem to be hundreds, maybe thousands, of variants of the colour green, from the brownish greens to the yellowish greens, and the silvery greens that sparkle deliciously in the wind, and all the greens that are extremely green, essentially green. All of it is growing, there's no doubt about that. It looks nice, and also it's a little unsettling. He is the shepherd of these plants, temporarily. The idea, as he gathered it, is to maintain their health, to favour what, among them, is good for humans, and eat what is edible. And if there's too much of that, he can give some to the neighbours, who, he was told, are very nice. And if there isn't enough, he can go to the market. Once this mental overview of his situation with respect to plants is complete, he stops thinking about plants, and focuses on his nose, or rather, on breathing through his nose. He inhales one deep breath, and notices there are a bunch of smells. He exhales powerfully, and the trees are very high. He is here. He has taken a few steps outside, in the morning, with his coffee, and has looked at the garden. It happened very naturally. It'll probably happen again.

A VISIT FROM JUDITH

He called Judith because he had a question about anise, not an essential question, really, he wanted to know whether it would be a good idea to marinate it in pastis, and she said absolutely, the idea is excellent, and she could show him something he could do with plants from the garden and pastis, if he wanted, and she could pop by in about three hours. He thought she probably wanted to see him in his new house with his new garden around him, and he'd been rather impolite to not invite her himself; she is, after all, his introducer to this obviously hallowed part of what was, for him, only "the south" before meeting her, and to the couple, and to the house he's living in now. But after all it's only been four days, it isn't that bad, and now she's coming: all is well. And he went back to work, like an automaton.

And now, about four hours later, he still hasn't made more coffee because he was thinking he'd make some for her when she'd arrive, but at 4 in the afternoon, it's almost too late for coffee. But not quite. And he hears a car arriving on the road and slowing down, and he knows that it's Judith, even though every car that passes through here does that and he already felt that it was Judith three times before, but this time, it really is her. Or at least he hopes it is, because the car is parking in front of the house. And he hears Judith's voice, the voice of Judith, producing a sound whose meaning is "anybody here?," so it is, in fact, Judith.

He screamed back, and Judith entered the kitchen, a place he has chosen as his working station despite there being a desk in the living room. As she comes in, tall and powerful and slightly mysterious, with a basket in her hand and a smile on her face, he realizes how happy he is to see her. Relieved, even. Her jawline is hard and powerful. Her skin is a vibrant reddish brown. She seems happy to see him as well, though he can't imagine why that might be. In any case, it's nice seeing someone, having a friend. It's been four days since he's seen anyone, and those were the happy couple, when they gave him the house keys and left him there, and the people who work at the supermarket in the town nearby. He hasn't seen or heard from the neighbours, those whom he was told were nice. Judith brings with her a slice of a pie she's made, which is nice; he offers her coffee and she says yes, but only a drop. It's strange to think they've lived together. Their interactions are full of smiles but happen as though they were from different species. She laughs a lot about him, in an affectionate but gently mocking way- she already did this when they met on the train, but their conversation then had been deep and fascinating (to him at least), whereas every conversation since has been pleasant but superficial. Still, there seems to be some genuine link between them, hidden under the smiles. But now they're in the garden, drinking the coffee and eating the pie (Judith laughed when he offered to go outside, it's a Parisian thing to do apparently), and they are talking. Judith is a rather mysterious person. She doesn't talk in much detail about her life, so he can only guess at what it might look like- it seems very full of things, very connected, both to people and other entities too, and also full of movement, mostly short trips within and around this region. The rhythm of her life is connected to other, larger rhythms, that of the seasons of course, and it is marked by regular events, regular meetings, within which or between which she seems to exercise an absolute form of freedom, an openness to whatever may come- the same pliancy that made her accept the arrival of this man, himself, into her life. He knows neither the rhythm, nor the freedom, and wonders how come this woman is so far above him in terms of how well she lives. Thinking back on her, he'll conclude that she has the ghost (the same ghost he has), but also something else. She explains things about plants that he mostly doesn't understand- mostly, it's the enthusiasm that he likes, and the idea of knowing about plants. They spend a nice moment, unconstrained, quite relaxed. She can come back tomorrow towards the same hour, if he wants. Of course he does.

THE FLOOR IS HAIRY

Judith left at some point, and he found himself thrown with some inertia on the path of words and communication, but with no humans to direct this hunger for expression to. So he calls a friend, one of his best friends, bothers him from his Parisian life, and recounts everything enthusiastically. The friend is curious and understanding, but also somehow withdrawn, almost mocking; they now speak from two different worlds. On the phone, behind his friend's voice, were the sounds of the city: ambulances, cries, horns blaring, and an overall rumble of activity. The friend probably only heard his own voice, and maybe some bird cries and chirps. Some people get annoyed by bird voices on the phone.

After the phone call, the afternoon is ending, and the night is almost here. The sun is almost not here anymore, which is almost scary; a childhood fear of nightfall that he had forgotten about is being reborn, here in the country. And his lust for communication and human contact still isn't satisfied, and he feels incapable of working now. He hasn't been anywhere near the plants all day, although he knows, in theory, what he must do to care for them and integrate them in his daily diet. There is something between the theory and the rhythm of his everyday movements that hasn't fallen into place yet, that demands an adjustment, maybe even a break; he hasn't gotten to the breaking point yet.

So he goes out into the garden, walking slowly, looking around, and his body and stature and the rhythm of his step and the frequency of his thoughts are all obviously, painfully detached from the atmosphere that is created and shared by all the plants, the silent trees with their rough wide trunks, the rustling trees with their sleek thin trunks, the low grass, the high grass, the spaces behind trees that have already disappeared in obscurity, the innumerable insects he knows are here, everywhere, the birds, etc. All of it is like an ultra-HD background image, but with smells and weight to them, and so, something theoretically real; but since he has no pattern for approaching this realness, he does what he knows: he walks slowly and watches, like one does in a museum or in a foreign city, a body, quite distinct from the scenery it is moving in. He doesn't think there is any other way to be among all this life, but the idea or impression that there is (a way) is already germinating in the depths of his conscious intelligence, beneath or above all of it, invisible still but there already, growing. His body is small compared to the trees and the hill on the left, whose verticality he can feel in his bones. His feet, lodged inside their very clean red cloth shoes, are shaken by a fearful spasm each time they come into contact with the extremity of a plant.

It is the evening, and in the evening energy goes down. So his head hangs forward, just like the head of certain big flowers hang when the stem is tired, and it isn't that his stem is tired, but there is a certain confusion in his relation to this bustling of information, both heterogeneous and homogeneous, all the same and different every time, the trees all unique but all very tree-like, the plants that are each individuals, and apparently so diverse in their behaviours and effects on human bodies, but who are also all acting more or less the same, and aren't saying anything. And all these things, unlike him, eternally keep pointing upward, wanting to go up, and indeed they go up, they grow, as much as their genome (or something) allows them to. There really is a thing that is coming from the ground, the heavy and relatively flat ground where we all stand, and that is going up. It would cause him anxiety if it weren't so exhausting, but it is exhausting, so he lets his head hang a little and walks, watching what is before his eyes with perhaps excessive attention, very much like a machine, not very conscious of how his body is feeling, nor of what he is doing, or what he would like to do; his head is heavy like the fat head of a baby on a tiny and soft baby body, and hanging toward the ground, and he is looking in the direction that this bending of the neck offers, that is, the ground.

The ground here isn't like the immaculate lawn his parents have in their house in the suburbs. Here, there is more sun, and not many people want a lawn anyway. The ground is covered in plants that are either hard and bunched up, and prickly, and immortal, or stubby, strong plants, with tufts of grass all around; or else it disappears under bushes of green plants that are edible or, at least, that you can do things with. Then there is the ground where people walk, where he is walking now, and that ground is hard, and you can see the bare earth with stones of varying sizes, roots sticking out of the ground, very hard roots sticking out of the hard compact soil, and some yellowish-green tufts of grass. So the ground is hard and hairy. And he, passing slowly over this ground, the ground where you walk, where you see the soil and stones, with a mind dizzied by this circumstance, notices only one thing: the ground is hairy. There is something exhausting about the observation. Or maybe it is exhausting to realize you've arrived to such considerations, and a certain languor in the air, or a certain hardness in the ground, or a moment in time where you need to forget yourself with something and cannot, to make this the only possible consideration to exist in one's mind, or intelligence, brain; head. And it isn't a charming idea, not even a fertile one; it is, itself, hard, infertile, slightly hairy, and this hairy hardness tickles the mind in a way that contains the potential to become unbearable. And so, he somehow finds a semblance of energy, interrupts his slow bent-headed walk, and goes back, with long fast Parisian steps, to the house, to the kitchen, and turns on the light, and stays there for a while, standing, wondering what exactly he thinks he's doing here.

A BOOK IS FOUND

He has been walking aimlessly about the house, stunned by the vastness of it (of it all), disoriented and vaguely creeped out by how cold the tiled floor now seems, and entering and exiting rooms without paying enough attention to them. If he could see himself as he does all this, if he was able to become aware of his movements and thoughts, he would be amazed at how much his course of actions resemble that of an ant, surprised by the moving of a stone nearby, and running about in every direction. But he can't, and he isn't. So he goes in, looks around, and the only impression he gets from everything is one of strangeness, oldness, humidity and solitude.

One of the rooms though, cold and high and old and alien like the rest, has a door in it that leads to another room. And that other room is a small one, where the bed is simply a bed; it doesn't have huge wooden panels or bars of iron decorated with old-fashioned designs like the others; isn't unduly high and doesn't have ornate feet; it is a bed, and the only thing it says is: I am a bed. It must be an IKEA bed. And it takes up much of the cold, tiled floor, and it is flanked by a pair of simple, reassuring nightstands. And next to the bed, there is a small bookshelf, like there are in most rooms in this house. But the room here is cosy and reassuring, and it doesn't have too much empty space to defy him, so he sits on the bed, and looks at the books. The books here are antiquities, bound in leather and fabric by devoted great-aunts; there are books about fishing, and books about hunting, including colonial-looking books about hunting in exotic places. There are also books of regional poetry that concern this region specifically. And in between two such books, there is one that stands out, but discreetly, because it is bound in pitch-black leather and it is very thin and tall.

He picks up the book, whose cover and spine are unmarked, and opens it. It cracks open like it's the first time someone has ever opened it. The first pages are blank. He's starting to get the impression that the whole book is blank. But the third page is printed with a title, in thin black letters: SCHERZI. And then, at the bottom of the page: 22/7. This seems home-made, but well made. The text is printed in traditional black, and there are etchings printed in black, except for one in the centre which is in red ink and seems interpolated, from another hand and another time. As he reads, not paying full attention, leafing through and stopping when his attention is piqued, he becomes disappointed: he doesn't understand. The text consists of dream accounts it seems, with out-of-place elements and brusque changes of setting and characters. There is one narrator though, and most of the accounts consist of people or groups of people gleefully showing that person something very specific, of high interest to them, but completely cryptic and undecipherable to the narrator and the reader. The illustrations, on the other

hand, are impressively well-drawn, but his apprehension of
them doesn't (and can't) go any further than that, because
he has no context for what they represent; the text is too
cryptic. There are snakes in every drawing, and owls in
most; all of them represent characters, either human or
humanoid, directing their attention at something outside
the frame, or things like skulls or snakes burning on altars,
or death itself, reading from a book. The central one sticks
out, though: it shows a canoe in a red swamp, gliding slowly
and silently on the water. In the canoe, a young Native
American man with a sharp nose is paddling, but looking
at the viewer; The sky is hidden by the dense foliage and
tree-trunks barring the background that falls down from
above, but nonetheless, it is the sky that carries the weight
of the drawing. It is a thick, red sky, and takes up almost
exactly half the page, disappearing into the foliage from
about the topmost horizontal third of it. The drawing is
slow, ponderous, silent and haunting. He closes the book.
A mind has amazing ways of forgetting about something
inconvenient. He simply leaves the book on the bed, for
what reason he will never know, and walks back out of the
room. He has made the decision to suck it up and prepare
himself some food.

WHO IS JUDITH?

It is another evening, a week and or so after having
found the book. He has had an early dinner (onion soup),
and is lying on his bed. Usually, lying on his bed and doing
nothing, or reading, is his favourite thing to do; his own

idea of a good time; the best time. But he is restless. By now he has started taking care of the plants, but there are less of them. The weather is becoming harsher. The trees are becoming bare. More and more, there are smells of burning things in the crisp air, especially in the evening; He doesn't know what the other people are doing, but they are doing it without him. Also, he is perpetually horny. He turns to the window and sees trees, their branches whacking each other with violence, leaves falling. Behind them, there is the hill. The sound of the wind is powerful. It seems that his kind ghost has become an armour now; in a sense it persists, because he hasn't snapped out of whatever it was in the way he had snapped into it, back in the caribbean. But it is changing. It was light and luminous; now it has grown heavy, is weighed down by something. It used to absorb his own sadness and angst, and dissolve them into joyful nothingness- and it also did the same for outside influences. Resolved them. Now it has grown harder, not hard like metal, but gooey, for now; and coloured, as though tainted. It does not fully absorb the sadness that is welling up inside him. It is, in fact, becoming saturated with it.

He thinks of Judith often. She brought him here. She is so free, so powerful, so independent and radiant. He wishes he knew her life, and could replicate it for himself. Maybe his dream of a house and fires wasn't that attainable after all. He has it, but it is too wide for him, and too alien. Judith knows this life. The outside world has brought him, through a series of mundane miracles, to this, his dream. And it doesn't fit. Or rather, he doesn't fit inside of it: it is too big for him.

Again, his mind circles around the idea of Judith, and her powerful teeth. Judith smiling. Judith taking care of things. Driving around. Appearing and disappearing. Her modern car; her knowledge of symbols. The wind is so loud, and this house is so big! He turns around, turning his back to the window and to his tea on the bedside table. He cowers. His thoughts are cluttered and clumsy, they start and stop, and another thought comes around, seemingly detached from the first one, though in reality they all spring out from a single thing, which to be concise we might call his mood, and it's a bad one. One of his hands dangles gently from the bed, and the other is clutched around his genitals. He falls asleep.

The following morning, he fumbles for his phone on the table: it is 8 o'clock. His cock is extraordinarily erect—filled with blood to capacity—hard as a rock. Bits of his last dream hang around in his mind, mixing with his perception of the cold room he's in, clinging to the asperities of perceptible reality, and also manifest within it: his cock. He remembers it was Judith, but also not her—more like a statue, a bronze statue like in the Prosper Mérimée novella, la Vénus d'Ille—in the dream, she was heavy, powerful and slow; she crushed him between her thighs, and crushed his bed, and crushed his house with her weight. Now, wide awake and with an erection, he wonders whether he is allowed to masturbate, and, moreover, to masturbate with this dreamt-up bronze Judith in mind. He decides against it. Still, as he drinks his coffee downstairs, his cock still thicker than at rest but now hanging loose, puffs of impressions from the dream come back to him, even whole images: Judith was a slow, bronze statue, her thighs thick and heavy, and her hair was hanging down heavy like chains around her still, powerful face. Her arms each weighed what his whole body weighs. She was naked, and cold like bronze but also somehow hot inside. And the presence of her was intoxicating, exciting to the point of madness, of veins bulging, heart pounding everywhere in his body, short breaths, sweat in the scalp. She came close to the bed he was in. She sat astride him. He couldn't breathe, both because she was so heavy and because he was so stimulated. And then the bed broke, and the floor broke, and he woke up. In the dream, the house was entirely tiled, from floor to ceiling, and the tiles were a cool green, and there were exotic plants everywhere.

EMPTY, BARREN, BEREFT

When he was younger, a teenager, there was a phase in his life where he listened to black metal. There was a music shop near his school, and he would go there, and choose the cheapest CDs with the scariest visuals, and then he would go back home and listen to them, sitting next to the radio, following the lyrics in the booklets that came with the CDs. After a while he fell in love with one band in particular, called Marduk, which he felt was somehow the purest in its wrongness, its evilness.

He would sit and listen, and feel a sense of unleashed power living inside his belly, echoing the steady and theatrical violence of the music. In the lyrics, words occurred and re-occurred, words like night, black, darkness, desecrated, demon, shadow, buried, sacred, that deeply satisfied him. He felt strong, and also he felt other, distinct from the world he was forced to inhabit. Not just different: the enemy. The feeling comforted him.

He has moved on from this period as he entered adolescence proper, and started to long for more gregarious pleasures, like parties, and the promise of sex that they offered. He started to wear coloured clothes, and his demeanour adapted to his new goals of impressing and seducing others. Later, he never deepened his interest for this style of music, except for short sessions, interspersed throughout the years, where he would return to the same albums he so religiously followed the lyrics of as a late child, sitting on the floor in his room. He would find them again on Spotify or Youtube, and google the lyrics, and reproduce the same mode of listening. Mostly the music seemed too harsh to his ears, now used to enjoying less saturated sounds, and the lyrics, childish, and he laughed at his past self- but sometimes, the old feeling came back, that of being the enemy, of moving with a great powerful darkness, adverse to the diurnal banalities of life, adverse even to the gregariousness of his city nightlife. He let himself savour the feeling, its power, how reassuring it was. Then, in the end, he'd laugh at himself and go back to his life. When confessing, in a social situation, to his black metal phase, he would mention how experimental the music was, and present it as an interesting artistic foray into the archetype of darkness and evil. He wouldn't mention the dark, adversarial feeling he got; indeed, he would forget about it.

Today, as he walks on the low plateau which is on the road side of the house, through seemingly dead plants, the feeling comes again, separate from the music. The night is starting to fall after what has been a grey, slow and silent day, and the sky gets its first colours on one side as the other steadily darkens. Dead trees rise toward the sky; dry herbs sway in the wind. The calm is deathly, and the mounting obscurity excites him. In the distance, he can see the hill that is occupied by a game farm, which has bared an entire side of the hill and covered it with nets held up by poles, to contain the grouse and geese they breed. There is a dog kennel behind that, at the top of the hill, and now, as often, the dogs are all howling, adding to the gloomy ambiance. This wintery scene, as the night falls, seems to him the materialization of the feeling he got from the music, and he gleefully basks in it. Then he laughs at himself, still quite evilly, and goes back to the kitchen to prepare dinner.

A VISIT FROM HALF THE COUPLE

He was sitting in front of the house, looking up at the branches above. His eyes were looking at the branches; his mind was trying not to recoil disgustedly from the sight. He could see that the branches were almost entirely naked, this is November, and that there were cold bits of white sky in between them. They moved slowly in the wind, oblivious and on a different plane entirely; he watched morosely, his mouth twitching without knowing it, unthinking, with a mind best defined as flat. Quite flat.

He was sitting there, with a flat mind that was fighting back against a mounting feeling of disgust, when a car arrived in the driveway, and the sound of it produced terror inside his belly, and outside, nothing.

He stays there, sat on a chair, looking up at the naked branches that jostle each other. The car stops with a pebbly sound, the motor stops, the door opens, pebbly steps, and the door closes. He doesn't move. His mind is flat. Then a voice is heard and it somehow becomes impossible not to react: "Yes, I'm here!!" he screams joyfully. This half of a couple is the beautiful half; it is a beautiful man that walks up to him, smiling widely but not in a way that might make one uneasy. He is smiling for real. He wants to know if everything is OK- it is, of course, what a wonderful house, I love it here! The interaction should be resolved by the exchange of pleasantries, and now we can get to the point.

But no. The man looks at him with his big beautiful eyes, and in the most compassionate yet not patronizing voice, he says something to the effect of: don't worry, the house takes some growing into. And then he speaks of other things, making any reaction impossible. This man seems to be of a vibe-sensing persuasion, and not only that: he is able to sense vibes and try to make them better if they are unpleasant ones. He is soothing and sweet. His name is Thomas. They drink tea together, and Thomas is visibly trying to act as a visitor to the house, and not as an owner. For his part, my main character is intentionally making references to the fact that this is more Thomas' house, to unburden himself from the responsibility of being the host. Thomas comes now, to his mind that was fighting abjection, as a warm wave of comfort: a wave of butter. He wants to roll in it. They talk about the house and then about their jobs, which are similar, in a sense.

Thomas then asks if there are is any news from Judith. No, he answers, Judith has disappeared from my life; and I miss her (as he says that he misses her, he remembers, in a flash, his dream where she was a statue that drove him mad with lust and crushed his bed and house)- I wonder where she is now. And of course, Thomas knows where she is. She has gone to a more mountainous region just north of this hilly region, as she does every year, to prepare her plant products with the other women in her group of harvesters, and to organize concerts. Oh really!, He says. I had no idea Judith organized concerts. Oh she certainly does, says Thomas. She's a folklorist and musicologist. Well who knew, he thinks. Thomas is surprised that he didn't know this, but no matter. He shows him where they keep the dried plants: there are big earthen jars in a room in the back of the house. The room is a workshop, and smells of grease and old metal, but when Thomas opens the jars, they are filled with piles of dried plants, greyish-green in tone, crisp and light between his fingers. The dried mint is the best; and he leaves his head above the jar much longer than a polite smell would require. The smell is sharp yet sugary, stinging his nose like pepper, but also deliciously warming his nostrils. It is a very green smell, a deep and rich green that is at once transparent, like water, and intense like something from which the water has been subtracted entirely. The smell speaks of water, for whatever reason, but dream-water, deep subterranean cave-water, bronze water, spicy water that wakes the mind. The mint is the antidote to how grey the trees are becoming now the sky is visible in between their naked branches. He makes a conscious effort to remember, the next time his mind becomes blank and has to fight back against the abjection of the falling winter, friendless and in a strange land, he must go back in this room and smell the mint, with his whole nose.

The handsome Thomas and him go back to the kitchen, where they finish their tea. He feels almost in love with Thomas.

COLD

The soil in the garden has become hard. He wants to learn everything about plants, but that'll have to wait 'till spring. Most of the plants are dry and dead, and disappearing in the cold ground. What edibles are left are sad, winter vegetables, roots and thick leaves. He finds them sad. The trees are bare and grey now, and the river is sickly; and he can't bear to imagine how cold it must be. He sees fish in there, cold, slow creatures, grey in colour, with stupid, empty eyes. A few dark algae are being moved about in the current. He can hear wild boar rustling about in the woods on the other side of the river; they are probably trying to get away from the hunters, he thinks- he heard the gunfire earlier.

Walking in the vegetation here is much harder than it seems. There aren't any paths between the trees other than what the boars trace in their daily travels, and everything is covered in dense shrubs, usually hard and covered in thorns. There are also thorny vines hanging from trees, and the trees themselves are short, stubby and mean. He wants to go up the hill through the shrubs, though he should be working and has no real reason to climb the hill. It came to him at some point as he was idly strolling through the garden, just taking a short break from his work. Perhaps it was the cold and the greyness of things that got to him. He wondered how come we never sit on the ground or climb rocks in the winter; It's as though nature becomes disgusting for a few months in the year. Indeed, he found it disgusting, and frightening- but part of him also wanted to love this, to find it peaceful, meaningful, beautiful. So he stood by the river, trying not to let his mind merge with the sad algae he saw, constantly being pulled by the cold current. He looked at the dense vegetation on the other side, and the big rocks. What ever in the world does one do with all this, he wondered as he fidgeted with something in his pocket. This isn't particularly picturesque; in fact it is almost foreboding, like how a horror film shows nature. How come, in his dreams of living around trees and non man-made things, he never even once considered winter? He annoys himself.

So he decided to do something about it. It was just too much; he couldn't go back to the house now and work, even though he must attend a conference call in less than three quarters of an hour. But he can't. This is too annoying. He charges through the river, hopping gracelessly from stone to stone, and when he gets on the other bank, he charges at the forest.

He ducks under vines and wiggles between trees; he seizes a stick and whacks at low branches as though to warn them. This is a fight. He has the sense to find a boar path, where progress is easier if you duck down to their height. All around, things are a blur of brown and greys. There are 1 or 2 meters from the river bank to where the hill really starts, and he gets there fast, fighting valiantly- but then the declivity becomes so steep that he needs both hands, and has to leave his stick on the ground. A swell of bravery takes over his body. He firmly grips the trunks of two baby trees, and pulls himself up. I can do this, he thinks, as he pants and lets his clothes be torn by the branches. His hands and feet aren't enough, he has to use knees and hips, elbows and shoulders, to bring himself up in certain harder passages. His disgust for the decay of things is no longer; it is replaced by his stronger will to get up there. There is no going back down anyway. He wants to make it. He will make it. His forehead becomes sweaty; a hot rage drives him on up the hill.

The road above the house is maybe 20 meters up from the river- he gets there fast. There is a short, stubby wall between the shrubby hillside and the road, which he climbs. When he appears, he sees a flash of orange vests, and hears a scream. He ducks down, instinctively, and then looks up: there are men in front of him, a few paces away on the road, standing by a white utility car. They are holding guns; and one is in front of another, his arm outstretched as though to stop him, as the first lowers his two-barrelled gun. The screams continue, then subside- it seems the man who was in front of the other just saved him from being shot. The men laugh now; all is well that could've been catastrophic. Every year, hunters kill donkeys, horses, dogs and even other humans that they mistook for game. He was almost the victim of one of those stupid mistakes, almost made into a statistic and a tragic local story. But he wasn't. He is afraid of these men, but they are talking to him now; he has no choice but to stay.

THE HUNTERS

They are all standing there near their white utility car, with their guns in their hands, and wearing fluorescent orange coats on top of their green, brown or black coats, made of ugly nylon material. They are men from the village, he knows, for those are the only ones that are allowed to hunt on this hill. They are laughing now, and saying he's lucky, he might've been shot. They don't say they are sorry: he does. He is still shaking a little bit, and a nervous erection is getting started inside his pants (who knew? If he was thinking he'd be finding it poetic)- he's very sorry, he didn't know, he- They are bewildered by his appearance. What was he doing, climbing up that hill. He eludes the question; now he's standing in front of their car, which contains the carcass of a boar that is being butchered. Blood everywhere, black and red. Red and blue internal organs. And a smell- not a stench, a pale viscous smell with a metallic twist. The men are mocking him; what a city boy, they say, what a foolish city boy, in their southern accents, look at how scared he is now. A few men are standing back a few feet, smoking cigarettes, pipes, and tiny, stinky cigars. He doesn't even try to be jolly or engaging, as he normally would, uncomfortable city boy, intimidated, unnatural boy. He is terrified still. He might've died, and his quasi-murderers are now laughing at him for putting himself in front of their guns. They offer him coffee, which he accepts, as the man who was butchering the boar resumes his work. They talk about accidents happening in the past, shots being fired at dogs and farm animals; he hardly listens. The trees are grey, and the road is grey, and the coffee is very bad. They now ask him some questions about himself; and they know much more than he would've thought. This isn't Paris, people talk. They know where he's from, and who introduced him. They know Judith; don't seem to like her much. He says thanks for the coffee, I've got something to do, and then he's on his way- he uses the road this time, a longer route but also safer.

VALENTINE WRITES A LONG EMAIL

The gist of it is, she's not over him, not over them being a thing. She's seeing other men but he's still the one. Not much has changed, except she's thinking more and more, she says, about ways in which it would be feasible to come join him. He answers that he'd like that.

ON THE ROAD TO THE LAKE

It is cold outside: the trees are passing by rapidly. It is early in the evening still, but also early winter, and the night is starting to creep into the corners of the general area on one side, as though plunging all things in an equally applied, dark blue ink. On the other side, the sky is pink, purple and orange, and delirious white on top of that, and the sun is a fat ball of orange light piercing through the clouds. The sky is wide, and the beauty of it is wide also. A wide beauty. Magnanimous. Riding at the back of the couple's car, he reluctantly feels a gushing of joy, or something like joy, in his stomach- maybe hope? The road is empty, passing through wide hills that are like fat round blobs of soil covered in trees like tight flocks of green sheep; an occasional pine tree catches the eye and affirms that this is the south, that we are close to the Mediterranean sea, where Greeks used to get marooned on mysterious islands that are now not much more than tiny rocks.

The atmosphere inside of the car is warm and mellow, and he feels warm, dressed in dark tones. He feels elegant. His black pants have exactly the right fit; they let him feel his own body as though he were naked, and also protect it from the mundaneness of the outside world; The car seat is a normal car seat, but right now, it is markedly inferior to his pants- their cut, their texture, their colour: a slightly washed-off black. His shoes are strong and lean. His socks are comfortable. He is definitely ready for this.

In the car, conversation is being had about this and that, and then about the people whose collective it is that is organising this party tonight. He has met them already, he is told, that other night at the lake. The lake was beautiful that night, he says. Oh, it was, they all agree.

These people, Thomas tells him, have a collective that is dedicated to nothing in particular, to good things in general- they do music events, theatre, a cooperative for agriculture, arranging paths for farmers to sell their products directly to their clients, or almost directly to nearby sellers, charity work, and, apparently, also sabotage. They also organize parties, like the one they are driving to. He doesn't think, as the list of what these people do is being enumerated to him, that these might be good people doing good things. He thinks about the party, how fun it will be, and maybe there will be people to seduce there. At the front of the car, they are talking about the Spanish contingent. He doesn't wonder who they might be. The road feels soft under the wheels of the car.

THE PARTY

It is a party. Music, loud and thudding. Good music in fact, arcane tunes, well articulated, weird, thrumming, wild and proud. Inducing craziness, or the feeling of lacking it. A general sense, as a result, of people attaining or having attained frenzy. Lights very low, low and warm or cold flashing white and powerful and then gone. Smoke everywhere. From cigarettes, from weed and from the stage smoke being spurted by machines, in long hisses. The music is very loud, throbbing. He knows this, and likes it- the laughing, breathless crowd dancing, the sweat, the smiles, the cries, people becoming mysterious, beautiful sirens for a while. Mythical beasts. But his body has become unused to this, and is shocked. Flashes of his trees, his garden, appear before his eyes. Soft and mellow, green and grey, cold, slow, dying- also beautiful, even under the low white sky. He longs for his garden; but not for his bed. He is happy to be here. Already he is slightly drunk. Soon he will be very drunk. People of all kinds everywhere, shouting and dancing. A few, that first catch the eye, are moving -one could say- radically, in a way that is free from self-consciousness. Some dance tribally- bouncing on the spot in a punk-rock way; some flailing and punching about like Nicolas Cage in Wild at Heart, and most just move a little bit, as little as possible, self conscious, looking around. And girls, more comfortable with their bodies, undulating with their hands up and fingers closed on the palm, not a fist but a closed hand, and teeth biting lips sometimes, eyes half closed, then eyes open, then smiling. He is not dancing; he never dances. Maybe this time he wishes he did though.

The couple are taking good care of him, they stayed together at the beginning and still form a unit, though they seem to know everyone here and he doesn't- they could have abandoned him, but haven't; he talked to people that talked to them and went his own way from there. Conversations, shouted on the dance floor or spoken outside, interrupted by getting drinks, coming across someone, needing to pee, answering the phone- conversations started, interrupted and resumed; a party is the essence of the social life, a fast and superficial version of it, and also more real; where it becomes most manifest- he already has a network of friends in the party, three boys that are very excited tonight, with whom he shared a playfully mischievous attitude at one point, a girl with black hair that is shy and yet provocative in her demeanour, that handsome guy who is friends with the couple, a woman who looks like Judith, but is not Judith. He told her she looked like a friend of his. She said is she pretty. He said very pretty. She said do you love her. He said maybe I do, I haven't thought about it. He was very elated and his form of speech then was closer to free association than everyday, thought-out conversation. He was surprised at what he said though, as though it were impossible now to take it back. It has now entered the outside world- it has been put into words.

There is a group of people that occupy the dance floor, are the energetic centre of it, younger than the rest, and most of them have black hair and tan skin. They are also wilder than the rest. They have clearly been taking pills of the exciting kind, since they are extraordinarily excited. There is a moving and fluctuating nucleus of them, that screams and dances and speaks loudly in Spanish. Girls and boys, some sticking out more than the rest (the butch girl with neon hair that dances like a warrior and her band of war-like friends, the slim mysterious girl that doesn't seem to ever smile but when she does, it is like sex, like the idea of sex in an adolescent's mind), and then there are the free elements, jumping in and out of the nucleus, in and out of the dance floor, going out and rolling joints, having conversations with locals. The Spanish contingent, someone says. He comes across some of them, in his own conversations with his ever expanding network of party friends. One jumps in between them and asks for a joint. One girl theatrically runs her hand through his hair and then immediately leaves, laughing loudly with her friends. He is unfazed. Very happy. He wishes he were the type that dances. He finished his beer, and gets started on the vodka.

Later in the night some of the people are gone, most of those that were on the fringes, having conversations -perhaps people more concerned with the other activities of the organizers, farmers, working people who have to wake up early tomorrow. They are the cold or tepid corollary of the party's hot centre, now most have left or are leaving, among whom some of his network, who he feels disappointed in, seeing now that they never had any intention to plunge in this, to get lost in this, they were just passengers, just stopping by; or perhaps worse: they don't like this party, they condemn it by leaving. But those are fleeting thoughts, the centre is still hot, and the fringes, being diminished, will now become subsumed by it, integrated to it. There are screams. Some faces he hasn't seen leave the dance floor once. A girl is having a cigarette and laughing, elated, her cheeks red. His network has simplified and deepened, a Spanish girl that was near the very thin and mysterious one has been with him for a good half-hour. Her name is Thaïs. They speak English, the lingua franca; she is the intellectual type but also drunk, and he finds her very pretty. She is quite short, has brown hair and a leather jacket, and very lively eyes. They have become very close, party close- they have chosen each other to some degree, at least for now. Her friends come by and ask her about things. She shows through words or movements that all is well, she's having a good time. His new party friends, passing by, have noticed that he had made a closer connection. Some looked disappointed, for many people go to a party hoping to make a connection, while others go hoping to forget themselves; those smiled or waved or made some joke.

At one point the girl had to leave for some reason, and now he is with one of the three mischievous boys he met at the beginning of the party and a girl who they (the three boys) knew from before. This boy is becoming sad as the alcohol gets to him, and the girl is taking care of him. He tries to help her, shows the boy the moon (full, once again) and the lake and the hills, in a rather trite and unconvincing attempt to cheer him up by reminding him how pretty the world can be. Look at how yellow the lights inside are, he says, look at how pink the dance floor is right now, isn't it wonderful that so many people are dancing, near a beautiful lake, under the full moon? He's never done this; this kind of Fellini monologue, it feels foolish to the part of him that observes silently, but that one is quite distinct from the part that is monologuing, trying to reassure the boy- this part is inflamed with alcohol and then discourse, with the poetry of things; with the beauty he's attempting to celebrate, and something in his talk seems to be working on the boy and his friend, because they are paying attention and not laughing. In truth, it is his enthusiasm that is enthralling; as soon as he concludes his diatribe, they start laughing at him and he laughs with them. He offers the boy and the girl a cigarette. He says I'll go get us a drink. He offers to go walk by the lake. They like the idea. The girl smiles at him.

As he walks to get drinks he gets a flash of Judith and what he said about her earlier. Does he love her? Absolutely not, he answers. Can a termite love a spaceship? But then again, he thinks, does a moth love a lamp?

Inside, there is a room that has been made into a bar, where drinks are cheap and surprisingly gourmet. Surprisingly gourmet. He waits for the hordes of excited or exceedingly relaxed requirers of drinks that were there before him to get what they wanted from the bar, then orders three beers (gourmet beers), and turns around to take in the room as he waits. The light is red and low, people become red skinned and demonic, with dark hair all, and hollow eye sockets. In a corner, Thaïs is passionately kissing a tall long haired boy. His stomach doesn't drop at the sight, that would be too much: it quivers. Like when you eat a hard boiled egg that was past the point of eating, and it tastes fine, but then it gets to your stomach, and your stomach quivers. He thinks he might feel sad; maybe even jealous. But the beers have been poured and his course of action has been decided in advance. He leaves the room, passing right next to the girl and the long haired boy. As he exits, she extends her hand out to touch his back. He doesn't turn. How strange.

The lake is beautiful at night, under the full moon. As he walks with his new friends, his mind again starts enumerating the elements that make up the perceptible landscape, adjoining to each the adjective: "beautiful." Beautiful water. Beautiful island. Beautiful white hills under the white moon. In the black sky. He and his new friends are joking about things, but he is deeply, uncomfortably, swept away by a thick wave of emotion. It blows his thoughts away like leaves. It shakes his legs. It turns his stomach upside down. He wants to cry. He wants to hug the girl and the boy. His emotions are dangerously welling up, he thinks, and turns away from the two others and takes a few steps toward the lake, in the same way a man who needs to fart takes a few steps away from the group he's in. He would like to stay calm and collected, but things are happening inside his chest and stomach; he whimpers. It was a discreet whimper, a contained one, but nonetheless. A whimper. The girl asks if he's all right. This triggers the well of emotion that he was keeping inside his stomach to well up and rise up and occupy all his chest, and come out through his throat, and come out through his face. He wails and cries. This is too much feeling. He crouches and puts one hand to the rocky ground, extremely surprised and also powerless. The rock is cold but reassuring. The girl and the boy are probably a little shocked; they come near him and awkwardly touch his shoulders, so elegantly clad in dark blue fabric. He had made himself so handsome, so unattainable, so strong. And now he's very near the ground, crying. It isn't even sadness, though, he thinks. But it's emotion, that's for sure.

A few moments go by like this, and he collects himself. He says to the two others he's sorry, he has no idea what just happened. They are cool about it. The girl actually hugs him. He is confused, and laughs through the tears. As fast as it had arrived, the thick wave of emotion recedes. He wants to joke and drink again. They go back to the party.

WILD HOGS

The party was great. There was that strange moment where emotions swelled up so violently in him, and seemingly unrelated to anything other than his aesthetic pleasure as he watched the lake, that he had to kneel. He doesn't remember having felt this since childhood. Later he noticed his short intellectual Spanish girl, Thaïs, not kissing a boy now but dancing; she noticed him too. He coldly went to speak with someone else he recognised because he was flustered and offended that she should choose to kiss another. She ignored him too, and he became angry and frustrated at how unjustly she was acting- inwardly of course, in a hidden way. But a few moments later she came up to him and asked how he was doing, obviously oblivious to everything he had just gone through in relation to her. He felt foolish, child-like, a mean, entitled, angry baby. But she seemed to fancy him still. They sat outside on a wall and talked, and laughed, and had inside jokes. Then, there was a moment of silence where her lips, especially the lower, more fleshy one, seemed extraordinarily present. Then they kissed; and it felt good. They kissed a lot, and after the kissing had heated up too much for this public space, she took him up to a room she knew upstairs and they kissed and undressed and touched each other's bodies in a hungry, enthusiastic manner. Then they had good sex. Not ecstatic, but good. Human. Respectful. They were very tender to each other after the first wave of desire was done, and when they heard Thomas' voice calling for him, wondering if he needed a ride home (what a perfect man Thomas is), they promised to meet again soon and exchanged contact information. Her name is Athenaïs, but people call her Thaïs.

Now he is back home to his lonely life which, though alleviated by having made contact with other people nearby, still feels like a mysterious burden. Not as much though. The area is now populated, in his mind, with more than mere ideas- hunters, farmers, plumbers- country people. There are a group of enterprising people organizing things; they have a big house by the lake. There is the Spanish girl, Thaïs, and the Spanish contingent. There are the others he met at the party. He enumerates his new connections in his mind as he inhales the cold night air.

He is wearing a fur coat he found in a closet upstairs; under that he is wrapped in two sweaters and a scarf. He is sitting outside, not even on the terrace but in the garden itself, and the night is dark already. The night is full of sounds. Cold sounds. Dark sounds. All of them, sounds that come from nowhere, because nothing can be seen except for the bright light of the waning moon, above the almost leafless branches of the trees, swinging gracefully. There isn't much wind. From time to time, a bird cries out into the night, a shrill call or a modulated hoot. He is sitting here because there is nothing else to do inside but read, or watch things on his computer. Or work. Why did he come strand himself in this cold, dark, empty countryside with no tomatoes in sight, no friends, no girlfriend? What inspired such a move? It was his ghost, he knows, though he would never admit to such a thing, to probably anyone he wasn't sure he would never meet again. He is ashamed. What kind of person believes he is miraculously wrapped in the robes of a ghost? Is this something schizophrenics do, something a mental disease inspires? He has been living with an imaginary friend, he realizes, quite simply. Like what atheists say believers do. He is worried about himself. Because, though he now chastises himself for having accepted delusion so wholeheartedly, he nonetheless recalls the various moments where he has perceived the ghost (or something), recalls them as actual memories, like the memory of his sadness at the party, or the last time he had sex with Valentine before he left. To his mind, he realizes, they are the same class of thought: memories. I remember feeling nothing when it turned out she had slept with that boy; I remember perceiving a distinct, delicious and painful texture upon every surface in our apartment. I remember driving and my car glided like the silver surfer's surfboard glides in between galaxies. Something triggered feelings in him, that became memories- accretions, life becoming story- within the flow of the rest of his memories, not distinct, not other; to his mind, they are valid phenomena. So why is he ashamed of recalling them as facts? It's not like he thinks he saw the virgin Mary, he thinks. Far from it. He underwent a change. No; something came over him- something alien and ethereal, something very discreet- and yet, something powerful enough that it derailed him. He is under the moon in a large garden with naked trees and tall plants that look dead, and birds are screaming. He had friends, and now they are far away. He had love, and he has walked away from it. He isn't on some kind of sacerdotal mission, isn't helping anyone, isn't finding himself particularly- in fact, he feels lost- so what is all of this? First hypothesis: he is suffering from a mental illness, maybe some type of cerebral vascular accident caused by a blood clot or something, that made him happen upon a subjective state of euphoria, accompanied by an underlying, lingering panic. This disease has made his behaviour unrecognisable and erratic and he is now his own enemy.

Or, second hypothesis: some kind of spirit (whatever that is), a nice one, has decided to ride him and give him peace. This has derailed his too comfortable life for his own good. For his own teaching. He must be curious and open to whatever happens because this is, in some way, being decided by a power that knows more than he does. The very thought of this offends his sensibility; he has learnt to disdain religion, magical thinking, and any mode of thinking that isn't aggressively, haughtily materialist. This line of thought he's just taken, the second hypothesis- it offends his very Frenchness. Descartes, not the actual philosopher Descartes, but the ideal Descartes that the French nation celebrates- essentially, a more scientific Voltaire, a cold and refined man, a seer of truth and contemplator of the beauties of reason, a man that coldly, righteously, dispassionately stomps on the base instinct that is the yearning for the sacred, Descartes is offended. And yet here he is- he laughs at himself. Or he would, perhaps, if truly he felt like he can inhabit this cold French stereotype of the Rational Man. But he can't. How is it more reasonable to disregard how he has described his own life to himself, for months now, not because he yearned for it, but because it simply happened- how is it more reasonable to condemn the feeling, or explain it away, explain his error in his interpretation of it? It isn't. And yet. The psyche of man is full of surprises, he knows. Things rise up from the depths; they make you act weird. Everyone knows that. But the very depths are not an observable zone of the brain. They are an idea. The depths... Looking back at the sky, he sees it has no depth when it is perfectly dark and cloudy, and the moon becomes hidden. It is cold, and the cold is starting to infiltrate the warm goose-down and wool shell he is wrapped inside of.

At his left, bushes rustle- it must have been loud because the sound startled him. He makes an effort not to move at all; all of his attention goes to his left ear, points to where the sound was. He hears a low sniffing, a guttural sound, like a groan, but a nose-groan, and a discreet rustling of sticks and leaves. Branches crack. There is something in the bush to his left; he is sure of it. Maybe several things. The bush is just a few meters away. Adrenaline has taken possession of his body already; his senses are wide awake, but also he is scared. What if it's dangerous? Wild hogs are dangerous, he heard- the hunters told him a story, almost mythological-sounding, of one of their friends being charged at by a hog, and his innards being laid out on sixteen meters at the end of which lay his motionless, lifeless, butchered body. A mother hog, of course, who was protecting her babies. He isn't interacting with any baby hogs at this time. But still.

To his left the rustling is continuing, and he can distinctly hear short, rhythmic breaths. They are deep and low, and nasal. The sounds sometimes seem to be getting further away, and sometimes they get so close he becomes paralysed, and he stays motionless, petrified, as though immobility might make an ill-intentioned animal believe he's just a log.

He stays petrified for a while; the snorts and rustles circle around, get harder to distinguish, but he is in a motionless state of flight; all of his consciousness is concentrated in his hearing (all he can see is pitch black where the noises come from, which is unnerving).

After a while, the sounds become more distant, then disappear. Still, he waits, making sure not to provoke a return of the beast, or beasts, with an imprudent movement. When a moment has gone by when he can't hear anything at all, he lets out a sigh of relief, and his senses start to function normally again- sound becomes normal, birds singing, wind blowing, branches clicking against each other creaks of wood. It is cold now. The sky is enormous and feels empty, like an empty eye socket, and from the hard, compact ground, the trees are hard and pointy like mean claws. There is life everywhere here, he knows; insects, small mammals, plants of all kinds. He is among them. Yet he gets up fast (his body is stiff and cold), and walks away to the house, once again beaten by the garden.

DID SOMETHING HAPPEN? MAYBE
NOTHING EVER HAPPENED

It isn't impossible that the hog was an illusion, after all.
Or hogs. Just as he himself was the illusion of a hog, and
then wasn't a hog but a confused Parisian man, panting
and slightly confused, emerging from a place from which
normally only a hog would emerge. He has changed rooms
in the house (there are so many), and has switched to the
river-side, the wild side, the cold side also, because it is
oriented more or less towards the north and the higher hill,
but now he can hear the tingling and white noise coming
from the river, and the naked branches banging against
each other, and owls and other beasts. Illusions.

Flashes of city feelings come back to him: when
suddenly it is spring in the middle of winter, and the sky
opens wide and the air becomes soft instead of sharp, and
the colours of things become visible, and for a minute you
get the illusion that everyone around is living a merry life-
you go out for drinks with friends in the warm air, and
somehow it's the best drinks and the best friends you've
ever had. A pair of eyes, as you walk down a street, that
goes up to you and then down fast again, as soon as it
notices you are looking too. Someone dressed in all purple.
A preadolescent face with skin so perfect it seems cut out
from a Botticelli. Cars pass by around the Bastille column,
with its shiny angel on top, and to the right is a group of
happy young people, and to the left are two bums fighting
disjointedly, and you are waiting for Valentine. How
Valentine appeared, how she appeared when he opened the
door to the apartment, at night, when he came back later

than her. The opposite configuration, when she appeared at the front door while he was doing something. They were always so happy to find each other again, every day. She appeared. Was Valentine real? He wonders whether he should ask her to come live with him, if that would make things better. Somehow he doubts it. A chasm has opened up under his feet; he still floats above it.

He has let time slip away from him tonight, without realizing it. Tomorrow is Monday, back-to-work day, and yet he is still wide awake in his bed. He can see a pale shroud of opalescent light in the mirror by the window: the still full moon, hidden behind clouds. The moon shines, the river flows, the trees rustle in the wind- this is what the non human world does all the time, it seems, while in the city so much always happens. He wishes he were inspired by all of this. He just wants sex and to eat good food, prepared by skilled chefs. He wants to be back in Paris, proudly floating about the busy streets, a man for whom the whole city is open, for whom the shops open, a man in the know, one who understands and is at one with it. Tomorrow he will wake up late and will be reprimanded for it by his hierarchy.

VALENTINE

Today, as he wakes up, the sun is weak but steady, and there are gusts of wind that pass over the house and his body, on the terrace, as he tries to work, but can't. He's thinking of Valentine a lot lately, he realizes after his thoughts have drifted towards her once again. He wonders where she is and what she is doing, though he also knows that she must be at work. He sees her in his mind's eye as in a movie, well-dressed and full of confidence, going about her daily life. He sees her hanging out with her friends, talking about life, flirting with boys at bars, reading a book in the sofa, driving to see her family, booking a weekend getaway with her best friend. Her life is elegant and natural. Nothing is forced or out of place. She, herself, is the living equivalent of 17th century neoclassical architecture. Elegant, mysterious, minimalistic, sculptural, harmonious, powerful, backed by power and history. He sees her face in his mind quite clearly today. Her eyes take on a special look when she is comfortable with whoeveUS troops r is around, or when she is alone. He thinks of those eyes, and the thought of them is now like a well into which all of his emotions can go and bathe. He loves her; he loves her so much.

BARTERING

He has invited Judith to an event, and of that he is proud. She has always provided all the opportunities, for as long as he's known her, and now it is his turn. Oh, it's not that much, and she might've found out about this and went without him. But when he told her about it, she hadn't heard that the Collective, who she does know about of course, are organizing a bartering event on the main alley of the town, a small town that is the urban centre of this rural area.

When they get there, though, she immediately is much more at home than he is, of course; people come up to her to chat, and she's the one that introduces him to them, grinning all the while as though the contrast between his power move of inviting her somewhere, and being the most present and connected one once there. Like ancient pagans to a sturdy oak tree, people flock to her to pay homage. They partake of her strength and power and then leave again, proud and rejuvenated, filled with a renewed faith in the goodness of things, of which she is a living proof- of health, of joy, of strength, and of the ability of humans to survive and thrive in this world. Or at least, that's what he thinks.

Looking around, he sees the street is quite different from how he has known it in the past- in the spring, there were old people sitting on benches and chatting, people playing pétanque, young people sitting on the top of benches with their feet resting where the seat normally is, and people passing by who were buying things in the city, sometimes recognizing each other and stopping to chat, sometimes walking to their car, sometimes slowly walking a dog or a young child. Then in the autumn and now the winter it was almost empty, with people going somewhere, almost exclusively, and everyone who before were drinking on the terraces of bars and restaurants hide away inside.

Today though, today the street is filled with people, more people than on market day, and different people, too. There are a great number of the type of person he would classify as hippies, or reggae-people, or professional circus people. Dreadlocks abound, and colourful but worn-out trousers that are exceptionally baggy, and rough linen or wool sweaters that seem handmade. Many tattoos of dream-catchers can be glimpsed on bare arms and legs, and rolled cigarettes and joints are ubiquitous. There are also people whose style and appearance is less expressive, whose hair, for example, is short, but still with an air of authenticity and grass-rootsedness that, in Paris, would have made him see them as decidedly other, and decide that his and theirs were different tribes and not meant to mingle. But here, they are at home and he is in their domain. They must be mingled with, and so he does.

He is trying to explain the concept of solarpunk to three hippies he has found himself in conversation with. There is a connivence between them, in contrast to what he is- they are gently mocking him. People here mock him a lot, he finds, but almost always gently. He knows other versions of him would have wanted to harshly combat this soft opposition, and belittle these pariahs, with their fingers plunged in the soil, far from the beating pulse of the city- at least inwardly he might've. He doesn't though- his is a position of curiosity and wonder, at everything these people represent that he does not. Solarpunk, essentially. He has the attitude of a student with the people he meets here, of someone who wishes to receive knowledge.

Still, there is him, one thing, and then them, another. Very different. He is now talking to one of the three he was being derided by, a young man in his twenties with a rugged face and calloused hands, and an aloofness that makes him appear wise beyond his years, and is asking him questions about permaculture. The young man is suprisingly blasé about the concept. He says he is more interested about true self-reliance, and the best means he has found to that end is not the perspective of permaculture, which he sees as an intellectual or a dreamers' ideal, but more traditional methods of organic farming. He is weary of novelty, of people who want to reinvent the wheel. He appeals to ancestors and people long dead, and says they didn't do permaculture, they did agriculture. He is interested, and knows it is not his place to debate the boy as an equal. He prods him though, wondering if the tremendous advances of science in describing complex systems and interactions between their parts, couldn't naturally give rise to new agricultural paradigms that are sustainable, moreso even than the old ones. The boy says yes, I know that's the idea, and I find it seductive too. As his deep brown eyes wisely consider the chaos of people before him, the boy references several books that he has never heard of. He has more to base his opinion on than him. And yet, it seems as though he is returning the boy to an earlier- or later- phase of his thought process about the whole thing. There is a dream that he has felt faintly, and the boy has felt intensely, that new knowledge could produce a radically different perspective, technologically less advanced, relying on the strength of a paradigm, and not on that of interlocking man-made conditions, to produce food and happy lives. The dream lingers.

The real, deeper question is the same for both- we are riding on the back of a terrifying monster- do we jump off? Do we kill the monster and use his flesh as fertilizer? Do we tame it? Their beers are finished and out of the corner of his eyes, he recognizes the dark whirlwind of the Spanish contingent. The loudest are speaking loudly in Catalan. There is Thais, among them, and seeing her jerks

him out of view of the colossal things the conversation
with the boy (Anthony) had materialized out of thin air,
before them. He wants to talk to her.

SEX

He has talked to her, and more: they drove back to
the house, his house, together, in the black daddy car that
came with the house. It has leather seats and a CD player,
with only two CDs: Born to Die by Lana del Rey, and
the New World Symphony. She chose Lana del Rey. From
the moment they started talking at the bartering event, he
knew and she knew, and she knew he knew and he knew
she knew- they were both thinking about sex. Two bright
pink lips, contained in her oval face; like jewellery; there
was an air of aggression around her eyes. She pursed her
lips. She was frowning. It wasn't ill feeling though; it was
intensity. His cheeks were flushed and he felt his belly and
cock awaken; he could tell that her temples were wet with
sweat, and her forehead under the thick black hair. She
hardly smiled as they talked, among the bartering hippies,
and her friends, the wild and manic Spanish contingent,
flitted by, in and out of the sub-continent they formed
there, talking. Talking, but what about? They couldn't
remember when they tried to, after having spent hard and
then ecstatic hours in his bed. Hard, and then ecstatic. Lana
del Rey in the car. The music went very well with what
both he and she knew was happening, and it is strange isn't
it, after all, how dark drama in sound resonates with drama
in bellies and veins.

He doesn't know that the New World Symphony would've worked as well though. Darkness. Hidden parts. Body parts, already throbbing. Bodies activated. Things become hard that were previously soft. They didn't pretend to be civilized, didn't have a drink of anything- they got straight to it, against the door as it was still closed, at first. It was his fingers inside her and their mouths breathing against one another, teeth banging, which he normally hates but the moment was special and this time it was nice- she could have chosen to lick his teeth and palate and he would've still been into it. They actually started having sex then and there, on the still closed shutter that leads to the kitchen, like adolescents at a party, and small strands of her black hair were getting caught in the splintering wood; but that didn't last for very long, because his arms became tired and the position was uncomfortable for her; he laughed and then she laughed and they pulled their pants up. She still had the furious look in her eyes, and he felt the same fury; the mundane turning of the key and opening of the door didn't change a thing about that, nor did going through the kitchen with her hand in his, and then climbing the stairs to his room.

It was maybe the first soft day of winter, still wintertime but mellow, with a warm blue sky and the birds were chirping. The room was warm and pale, his bed delicious; the old fashioned sheets were not soft, but rich and rough to the touch. They didn't start fucking immediately, though they wanted to- she got his cock out in a swift, humorous movement, and then it was above her belly for a while, where soft hairs descended from

her belly button to the cotton panties she was wearing-
his cock hovered and twitched above her as the smashed
their mouths together. She touched him, and there was
something scandalous and thrilling about feeling the intent
in her grip- and he touched her back. She was wet, like
a spring- spring was maybe returning. The sex this time
was long and exerting, physical, because they shook their
limbs a lot, and she sucked him and he sucked her for a
long time, and they caressed each other and pumped their
bloated organs together with ardour. When the ardour
was gone, at one point she had cried, and later he would
wonder why, though while it was happening he took it in
stride. They were both exhausted; no energy left in the
legs at all, and also dizzy. They lay for a while, and he was
thinking about his ghost and whether or not he believed
in ghosts, or in god, and about the Spanish contingent. He
was thinking in spurts, though, because the most present
and tangible thing at this time was the physical realm, not
the thoughts. It was his body, her body, and the sheets
in the bed. And the pillows. Her hair was all over one of
them, thin straight black hair, as her face looked up, no
longer angry now but dazed, herself, too, taking a moment
for herself after all that. When they were able they went
down, giddy and weak, and proud of the weakness in their
bodies- something strong had transpired between them.
He cut some dry sausage and cheese, with bread and some
pickles the couple had made and left there, and poured
out some wine, and they went outside, where night was
falling but the air was still soft and sweet like a prelude to
spring. The trees were still bare, and not a flower in sight;
they could hear the river flowing though, and birdsong.

The sky was brightly coloured and the moon could be seen through the branches of the high trees by the terrace. They ate voraciously and talked about the sex, and then they went back in. Turns out she is Mexican, not Spanish.

BATTLE IN THE SKY

Each night, after finishing his normal work hours, he has taken up the habit of going out and walking for a while as the sun goes down. As the days grow longer, his walks do so also, and he either eats dinner early, as the workday ends, or late, when the sun has finally set. He hasn't theorized much around his new habit, but has noticed this compulsion to go outside, more and more, and his sense of seclusion once he's back inside, and shuts the door. It reduces the scope of the world; at least of the world his senses can grasp.

Tonight, he hasn't eaten yet, but has come back from his walk earlier than usual, and instantly felt like an animal in an unpleasant cage. The lighting makes everything yellow at night, and it isn't a warm, pleasant yellow, but more of a dirty nicotine colour. Unable to stay where he is and start preparing dinner, he runs up the two flights of stairs to the second floor, and goes to lie down on a small tiled roof just under the window, taking care to distribute his weight evenly in order to avoid breaking any of the tiles. Lying here, he faces the direction where the sun is currently disappearing, has disappeared in fact, but is still lighting up the clouds and sky. This is on neither hilly sides of the valley but rather in the direction of the road and river, who run parallel to each other in an essentially north-south axis, in between the high and the low hills.

A great cloud is barring the sky diagonally above the horizon, heavy grey, that looks like a large whale. No he thinks- it looks like a very large bug, a flea, jumping up into what's left of the blue sky. Would my ancestors have seen it as a sign of some kind of flea-god? Is it a personal message for me? The presumptuousness of the notion strikes him at once: he's not the only potential witness to the shape of this cloud; many others must be seeing it right now, further down the valley. It could still be construed as a message to the valley, he reasons, since it is the focal point of the sky only from the perspective it (the valley) offers. The idea of spirits is seductive, and them manifesting through those phenomena of the physical world that are the least material is also seductive. Spirit shapes spiritual matter, thus establishing a link between its world and the world of matter and its inhabitants. Why not, after all? One feels unsure upon entering such paths. What madness might they lead to? But also, if he decided to try them as a psychological experiment, a mind-trick, an artistic exploration, then suddenly they become neutered, tolerable, he might even talk to friends about them. Also, as he engages in them, they feel no more or less dangerous than poetry does.

What for, though? There is no discernible message he can find in this giant jumping flea. As he dissects the nuances of grey, blue and pale gold, though, where the light part of the sky is, and contrasts the light with the shadow by looking at nothing in particular, just the sky in general, a feeling of delight emerges. The sky is erotic, for some reason. There is a tension, a softness and a beauty that are akin to the tension of blood-filled organs, the softness of skin and hair, the beauty of stimulation. He thinks again about Thaïs and the desperate look on her face as she chases pleasure within herself. She has a brutal approach to pleasure. It is intimidating and yet, there is nothing to be intimidated by, he thinks.

Looking up at the sky again, he sees the flea has now been flattened by the wind, and it has lost its flea characteristics. She now more resembles an Aztec divinity, in profile, those that look at you through the corner of their eye as they seem to dance. It is quite vague, but there is an Aztec head with a headband and open mouth there, on the right side of the cloud. Then there is the cloud, and at the other end, what used to be the jumping flea's leg, now becomes a pair of god's legs.

Right above the Aztec god, there is a narrow sliver of blue-grey sky, immediately followed by a sheet of indistinguishable dark clouds that cover all the rest of the sky all the way down to the horizon behind him, where night already covers the world. Turning back to the Aztec god, he sees it is moving slowly, as clouds do- calmly floating under the great dark mass, north-east bound, unbothered. It's funny, he observes, the Aztec god cloud seems to be much darker than the immense sheet of clouds that takes up the rest of the sky, though it logically shouldn't be. It is because, he reasons, there is light around it, while the huge cover of clouds is only surrounded by its own darkness, and so the dark in the Aztec god seems much darker by contrast. His mind wants to make metaphorical connections based on the observations, but he doesn't want to allow it. After a short thoughtless while though, it happens anyway.

The long floating cloud could be the sun god Huitzilopochtli, he thinks, as it is the lonely cloud that is leaving with the sun, the individuated cloud, and then the rest of the sky is Tezcatlipoca, the dark chaos, coming after him. The long cloud appears darker because it is contrasted against a light background, whereas the dark chaos is unindividuated, enormous, and incomprehensible. It arrives right on top of Huitzilopochtli's back, who streams on towards the right, unbothered. If he turns his head, he sees the chaotic all-covering cloud becoming the night sky, coming up from behind him. Before him, the sun doesn't seem to be leaving anymore; the light just stays and stays, providing a backdrop for the blasé Huitzilopochtli, who grimaces knowingly. Yes, these are the mysteries of night and day, of light and darkness, he thinks, now elated. But then he retorts: they are also the mysteries of illusion, powerful illusion that the mind clings to and that lead nowhere. He lays back, distracted from the unfolding spectacle by his reverie. When, after a while, he looks at the sky again, Huitzilopochtli has dissolved into a disjointed chain of clouds, his head and body fractured against the fig tree that is right behind the house; only his legs remain. His enemy, Tezcatlipoca, has receded and fallen away from that side of the sky, and is now much further toward the top of the sky, and also broken up, no longer threatening. There is a sense of something being over.

He gets back up, and as he enters the room, the constricting walls weigh on him exactly as much as before. He is struck by the dirtiness of the yellow light, by how dirty and humid everything is. So much for the mysteries of light and shadow, he thinks.

THAÏS KEEPS GIVING

It is nearing the end of the second week after their wonderful sex, and she almost lives here by now. She has chosen a room, her favourite, the one from which he has accessed the roof where he lay, from which he watched the great battle in the sky. It is a great luxury to have a huge house like this, with so many rooms, as extended families did in olden times; a luxury that is utterly inaccessible in Paris but feels natural in a remote place like this, whose remoteness is the condition for imagining wonders such as this.

They sleep together much of the time, but not always-sometimes, she comes to his room to have sex or read, or both, and then she goes back to sleep in her own bed. On other evenings, they have watched a film together and fallen asleep on her bed.

She is a mysterious one, with a sort of darkness around her actions, even around her smile. She is also a very joyful presence, because she is learning how to be joyful, she says. She has studied psychology, but is taking a long holiday in France. She'll be leaving in a few months. Her movements and facial expressions betray a profound and fiery internal activity, molten rock and great hollow caves, that doesn't seem to find expression in any other way than those passing signs- her conversation is open, and curious, her laughs come easily. In between those, though, her eyes will suddenly deepen, or her mouth will purse, or she'll put both her hands together on her knees and bend her head a little, letting her dark brown hair hang down across her temples. He doesn't want to try and resolve the mystery of her, though. He enjoys her presence. The signs of internal activity are not discussed. Perhaps no discursive means could bridge the gap without voiding its wideness.

She is an excellent cook, and likes his own cooking, while he was getting tired of it. The way she does things has nothing to do with his own way, and to him, this is the most salient cultural break between them, and a source of endless conversation. She, on the other hand, seems to think that everything separates them. The fact that they communicate in English, which is neither one's real, organic language, makes their relationship strangely formal, like an endless party conversation, light and superficial, continuing on without ever corresponding to the depth of sensation and emotion they can share. He feels like a coddled child when he guesses at what she sees when she looks at him, because her northern Mexican reality, though in no way exceptional or particularly tragic, is inherently harsher than his French one.

He has told her about the ghost and about the surges of eerie feeling that he has been subject to lately, feigning to trust her professional diagnosis as a psychologist. She also knows all about Valentine and their strange non-breakup, and how his life has become weird and unreadable since the ghost occurred. He knows much less about her; perhaps he trusts her more than she does him. He actually just trusts her because he senses she won't think any less of him because of his oddities. They aren't very odd to her, though she doesn't claim to understand them. She doesn't live a particularly magical life, or at any rate not in any obvious way, when looking from the outside in. It's simply that there isn't a break or taboo that separates normality from ghosts, in her world.

8 SPANIARDS

The Spanish contingent is here. They are loud and wonderful; much more organized than he would've thought when witnessing their chaos from afar. There was a moment where he, as the Parisian bourgeois he is, was afraid that the whole thing had been a scam, Thaïs only a lure, in order to find a new home for the whole colony. He was ashamed of thinking like that, but he did. And he still thinks that possibly, in some way, it is true- but without a doubt, not in the cold, calculated way his paranoia had imagined. In truth, the contingent is only here because they came to visit their friend and her new lover, and they felt such wonder at the place that they quite naturally asked if they could stay. Oh, you can stay, he said, laughing. And then, to his surprise, they did. Looking deeper than that, still, the contingent is a group of social surfers, whose philosophy, such as it is, is centred around their refusal to be "atomised", as they put it. They each feel augmented by the group and they find currents within the activities of groups they frequent that can sustain them, and that they can accelerate in return. The way in which they accelerate momentum for the sedentary groups they attach themselves to is because, as Esme, the theoretician of the group, put it: they are wild. The people they meet are civilized. They offer a bargain: their wild qualities, against their hosts' domestic qualities. The host provides shelter and roots.

They provide energy, in general, and also applied to all the particular things that atomised people must wait and delay for, because they are few and can't pool collective energy like the contingent can. Esme's thinking is like the marriage of Jack London and Karl Marx, he thinks. Seamless.

They are not looking for a place to found a community, Thaïs explains one evening as the others tend to various chores or lounge around. As she explains, it appears clearly that she is answering in advance to a series of Frequently Asked Questions, almost contractually. He listens: they are a moving community and will go wherever they feel they might have a good time, sometimes in exchange for something (together, they have a varied and interesting palette of skills), and sometimes in exchange for nothing but existing. They are not a part of the Collective. Just friends. And by the way, Thaïs adds, they do not call themselves the Spanish contingent, that's just what members and frequenters of the collective have dubbed them in this area. They don't call themselves anything further than "nosotros" or "la banda", or, ironically, "el gang", "la tribu". How nice that they had reason to name themselves, being a thing, and yet chose not to, he thinks. Even Esme's theorizing stops early enough to leave some empty space for the surprises of ever-unfolding present moments. That is wisdom, he reflects. They have been moving around Spain, France, and even Germany and Austria; losing and gaining members along the way, though the members that stick around are always either from Spain or from other Spanish-speaking countries. They have friends from all over, but strangely enough they never stick around enough to become part of "la banda", though one uprooted American girl they often refer to, Heather, has almost made it at one point.

He would admire their life in theory and practise, and wonder whether he should join them, learn Spanish and try and blend in, if he weren't so occupied trying to determine whether he is going crazy or not, as related to the religious implications of his ghost and subsequent weirdness. The way events are unfolding seems to suggest that he is, in so far is he departing from what is expected of him, among those who have known him the longest. He is becoming someone he and his friends back in Paris would possibly make fun of. His family wouldn't approve, either. Valentine wouldn't approve, he thinks.

VALENTINE COMES TO VISIT

At one point in an answer to an email, he had told her to come anytime she felt like it, if she needed a change of air, or if she felt ready to frequent him in his new surroundings. She knew about Thaïs, but not about the Spanish contingent, and she was surprised when she arrived in her red spotless rented car, parked behind the house, and saw a half dozen people with strange haircuts trimming the vine behind the house. Furthermore, she timidly arrived on the terrace just as Thaïs and a Spanish girl, Teresa, were anointing his lips with a mixture of brown sugar and lemon juice. It looked like the beginning of a porn film, she later said. A good porn film, though. Artistic. He knew she was coming of course, she wouldn't have dreamt of making it a surprise, but he didn't know exactly when, and her last message had been as the train arrived. If he had known, he would've tried to keep himself in a state of awkward inactivity in order to be ready for her arrival. But he didn't, and here she is. Thaïs, who knows the whole story and that it isn't over, says something incomprehensible to Teresa who says "Aaaa si!" and gets up, a quick "hi" with an almost convincing smile towards Valentine and then they both go into the house. There are other ways out.

Valentine is very much Valentine- that is, beautiful, and entirely unblemished, from her hair to her feet. There is an amusing contrast between her perfect outfit and her brand new rolling suitcase, and the organic patinas that cover every surface here. Even the gravel underneath her cute leather shoes is a little too rough. She is a star, self-designed to fit into cocktails before fashion shows, and out of place on the sandy gravel, between a wild boxwood bush and the planks of rough wood that are laid on the wall. The contrast of glamour with rusticity has been exploited by photographers before, but this goes further than that. There is something impossible about it, like a fish on a tree branch, like a rough copy and paste between two pictures that are entirely different in context, date and lighting. It is so shocking that he, weak man that he is, looks at her, wondering whether this can even work. He is a lowly creature, though. She is a real human and owns a warm, beating heart that she miraculously hasn't lost or interred along the way. She says hi to Jorge, Esme and Maribel, who are heading to the end of the garden with their yoga mats, with an unmistakably honest blend of natural pride and natural shyness, and then follows him, baffled, certainly, but also curious, to the kitchen, from which they go into the house and he shows her what rooms are left for her to choose from.

So where's your room, she asks, and he shows it to her. She likes it and says, here. He looks at her and she looks at him, and the frankness of the bond between them seems unaffected by the time spent apart. There is a kiss in the air, but also a question that leaves it hanging: what does it mean if they kiss? And then, the corollary: What does it mean if they don't? What does it mean if she sleeps in his room, or if she doesn't? What will Thaïs think? These are his thoughts. We don't know hers, but we can guess. Knowing her, she must be wondering which course of action will keep heartbreak at bay most reliably. She's a practical one.

Anyway, they kiss. They both weren't saying or doing anything except looking at each other in the eyes, so there really was no other option because, in those conditions, whatever questions are lingering in the air become fainter and fainter until they disappear. The lips and eyes and presence of the other is like a wind that undoes the question like clouds are undone by the evening wind.

They kiss, and it is more than nice for both. It is a kiss like remembering your favourite food as you eat it again after years of amnesia. Centuries. They kiss and kiss and also produce surprising grunts and sighs of delight as they touch and smell each other's face and neck. The level of intimacy that is currently re-arising between them is such that we must leave for now, as it is impossible to describe.

VALENTINE LEAVES

When they came out of the room, she was adapted to the place. Everyone loved her, and not just because it is easy to be loved when you are beautiful, with eyes that give you a false air of innocence and hypnotise whoever looks into them at the same time. Everyone but Thaïs. Thaïs hardly said a word to him or her during the three days Valentine was here; in fact, she hardly appeared at all after Valentine's surprise arrival. She and four others were taking out all the stones from the empty field and building a small hut with them, as people have done around here for millennia, as Esme explained, citing her sources just in case. When she did reappear, they were in the kitchen eating fava beans and cheese with bread soaked in olive oil. She casually said hi to both and then went back to joking loudly with Esme, Joanna and Tiny Pedrito. She said "Ah Tiny, no mames!" loudly and joyfully, boisterously even, and then laughed, but then almost immediately shot a dark look at the wall. Then she left. Later she would say of course I'm not jealous, and then, when prodded with more questions and demonstrations, would admit that she was, but didn't want to admit it because she doesn't want to "go steady" with him or anyone. Which is fair enough.

But all the rest were kind to her, and her stay smoothed something in her face that was becoming wrinkled and angry, that was visible to expert eyes when she arrived. He would like to think that he is the cause of the change, but also knows that he isn't. Just the vehicle; perhaps not even that. When she left, she was perfect and spotless again, but the contrast with the rurality all around was a harmonious one. She drove off and he felt his heart follow the car, which hurt as it exited his chest and then tugged at the strings connecting them. She said she would be back. She was surprised at how much his life had diverged from their life together, but pleasantly so. Almost as though she were waiting for him to build this one, to come in as the foundations of the dream were lain. He can't fault her; she clearly deserves to act so aristocratically- since she does.

SATISFACTION

Sometimes, you put an object of a certain texture and colour on a surface of another texture and colour, and it just feels right. Normally he wouldn't notice, but these days he notices everything. He can feel his brain, or rather, his mind, growing like the head of a mushroom. So when he tried to put the dark blue glass ashtray on the yellow blanket on his bed, he noticed it didn't work. Too unstable, and the materials were maladapted to each other. So then he put the ashtray on the flat, brownish-grey, rougher blanket, and it worked. It was extremely satisfying, somehow, and he relaxed into his inactivity, smoking an extremely light joint, because he is too sensitive to need much weed. He feels like a lion, in the sense that lions also lounge a lot, whether full or empty, and do not feel guilt or shame when they do so. His own laziness enchants him. The fact that his laziness enchants him instead of making him hate himself enchants him as well. He is an enchanted person. From his window he can see a rectangular cut-out of the garden and banks of the stream: green leaves all over, with spots of brown tree-trunks and a bit of yellow ochre where the naked earth appears on the steep hill. His excellent human hearing detects all sorts of directions from which all kinds of birds are tweeting, chirping, screaming and singing. Lately he has been doing nothing but noticing things, and going out of his way to notice some more. There seems to be no end to what can be noticed. This extreme attentive activity has been surprisingly tiring, and as a result he also has been sleeping a lot. He participates in activities with the others, but his rhythm really is his own, and only intersects with that of the group at convenient times. He is radiant, though, and people are noticing. They are starting to seek him out more, and he can only witness himself being radiant, and others seeking him out, with a radiant warm halo of joy and healthy self-satisfaction. Or at least it feels healthy. He's letting his moustache grow, too, something he would've been afraid of doing back in Paris, he surmises, and the moustache is also a source of endless joy and prideful looks in the mirror. It makes his whole body make sense, he feels, like for example the hairs on his chest, around his navel and on his limbs, that always felt out of place before. Pimples are disappearing from the parched white skin of his legs, as the skin becomes less white and less parched. His urban skin is becoming rural skin. This feeds into his discreet ecstasy.

Presently, as he lays on his bed, enjoying the effects of the weed on his hearing and perception of his own body and nibbling on pine nuts and pomegranates (the natural companions of weed, according to his new friends, citing Pliny) Maribel and Thaïs come into his room, followed by Jorge. His first reaction is to find them extremely attractive, and his second reaction is to tell them that, with mock sarcasm (that is, false sarcasm, or in other words, sincerity disguised as sarcasm). They giggle and return lavish compliments.

ELECTRICITY; FRIGHTENING CHANGES OF COLOUR, SITH POWERS; TECHNO

It is four hours later, and the pleasant lounging on the bed with his three friends has somehow become a foursome. They are having sex. Part of him still doesn't believe it, but most of him is simply enjoying it, for now, though the constant swapping of partners and positions is starting to make the pleasure deep instead of superficial, the athletic aspect more harrowing, his cognitive function more blurred and less complex, and the gusts of pleasure more brutal. The specifics are banal. But the overall sensation is special: to his shifted mode of perception, they are becoming not four people doing things to each other, but one beast in a current of power, stimulated to the extreme. Or a knot of serpents, writhing in unison, indistinguishable as individuals. He is losing himself in this, quite literally: the totality is what occupies his cognition. He is becoming scared, but also he could stop if he wanted, and yet he wants more. He has also lost, along the way, the sexual identity he thought was his, having engaged in pleasant exchanges with Jorge just as well as with the girls. Everyone on this bed is bisexual. Everyone is pansexual. Everyone is sex. It is all just stimulation, vertigo, and loss of bodily fluids, four open mouths, orifices galore, 8 hands, and spasms more and more. A purple tension, light, energy, or wave, is before and behind his eyes, burning them both hot and cold. Spikes of power, like beams of energy in heroic fantasy, are shooting up skyward from sweaty skulls. Ass cheeks and thighs start vibrating randomly- someone's leg kicks up. It lasts and lasts, too, all eight eyes and four mouths open as can be, everyone neighing like a horse or screaming like a person who is falling from a plane. Purple becomes yellow, yellow becomes red, red becomes blue, blue becomes purple. If there is such a thing as an electric wind, this is what is blowing here. The miraculous moment of orgasm, that often lasts for only a fraction of a second, is lasting for seconds now, maybe minutes; everybody has looks of painful surprise on their faces. Then it starts to slow down, and it goes back to a normal human orgasm; then it turns to slight pain. Then it is gone.

There is a glass bottle filled with water here, and they all drink from it, and drink the water from each other's mouths. Then they rest, a now immobile nest of serpents. Someone goes down and fetches some food. They don't speak yet; when they will, the main shared emotions will be joy, and incredulity. They will laugh a lot and eat, and then they will fall asleep together, proud and satisfied with how their day has turned out, deserving of some rest.

NO MORE JOB

He has quit it. It was the sixth-month assessment, and they said they were happy with his work and would like to continue collaborating, expecting his assent as a matter of course. He surprised them (and himself) by saying no, I have other priorities at this time, I have enjoyed my time working with you but I must take this occasion to suspend our "collaboration" (it was said orally, but with inverted commas only he knew were present). What other priorities was he referring to? He isn't sure, and they didn't ask. But it is done now. He is an unemployed city-dweller turned rural, living on a commune. Thank god his hair still looks normal.

VALENTINE COMES BACK FOR A WHILE

Thaïs and him are still friends, but no longer lovers, it seems. The intensity of their relationship has brutally lost its volume, as a soufflé does after having been left out of the oven a little too long. They are still friendly though, but not very intimate. There might be a pattern there, he reflects, as the situation resembles the way in which his friendship with Judith changed after the elated intensity and surprise of their first meeting. Maybe, he reasons, maybe I am a boring man who can only give off the illusion of being interesting the first few times someone meets me. Maybe the only real attraction a person can feel towards me is only sexual in nature ("only" sexual in nature, an inner voice cryptically objects, but the remark remains in the air).

In that case, he reasons, if he truly is so dull and boring, he is lucky to be at least somewhat attractive. Thaïs has a flattering way of looking at him though. Like a mystery whose key she thought she had found, and now lost, but whose wonders are still vivid in her mind. The sex they had was great; and that might be the extent of the mystery. Yet the pathway to their great sex now seems obscure. They tentatively circle around each other, knowing there is something there, but not finding it anymore, and then they return to the path they know, their respective inertias, which lead them rather apart from each other, though, possibly, against their will. The truth is, their will is hidden to them; revealed only after it has been made manifest by acts. Maybe that's why they lost the path to each other; maybe that's just the way things are.

When Valentine arrives again, she is again too spotless for her surroundings, creating an uncanny distance between everything and herself, like a goddess among mortals, or a Photoshopped picture among vivid ones; and then, after having disappeared in his room with him for a while, she re-emerges, having shed her mysterious city-varnish. People are glad to see her, and they joke and treat her with friendly complicity, which she reciprocates. She is also asking many more questions about people and their interests and areas of knowledge. She is trying to absorb their knowledge, he thinks as he witnesses her floating expertly in this unusual environment, which means she might be making plans to stay. He admires her ease, and the dynamics of her life. Things fall into place very elegantly for her. Once again, it is obvious to him that she deserves such elegance in the rhythm of her life, being herself, such an elegant being in all aspects. Her presence here feels like a treasure in his stomach, literally a small ornate box filled with gold coins and jewels, stuck in his belly. It hurts in a shiny sort of way. He is also experiencing a phenomenon whereby every time she moves, his belly moves in the same direction. Is This Love that I'm feeling? He wonders. Or is it just confusion?

VALENTINE AND THAIS

Since Valentine's return, the two have dropped their mutual standoffishness. You can see them gathering plants together sometimes. He was surprised to see Valentine show something on her phone to a giggly Thaïs, and later on, the pair sitting at the bottom of one of the trees by the river, seemingly involved in a deep, intense discussion. Later, when he inquired what they had been talking about, Valentine said "feminism". Thaïs said "things", and then laughed joyfully and looked down, as though angry at her shoes. One evening, as some were dancing while the rest talked and watched, the two danced together almost throughout the evening, and didn't seem to notice much when others attempted to participate in their fun by imitating their moves or displaying one especially for them. If he had been a dancing person, he might've tried, but he isn't, so he talked to Miguel all evening about sustainable architecture, and pretended not to notice them. All the rest didn't pretend, though. Valentine and Thaïs were becoming friends.

KOLKHOZE, KIBBOUTZ, COMMUNE

He wasn't sure how to approach the plants; they posed an insoluble problem once they had been abstractly invested with the power to feed, heal, balance and, more generally, make life better. Before that, they were things you walk on and chop off if they're in your way, and leave be if they're not. It was a satisfactory position, because he had no notion of another possible approach, apart from the ornamental one, which he considers to be nice, but a detail. This is different, it invests the herbs with individuality (as species, and also as individuals, now his powers of observation are maturing) power, and a history. Their multitude of names suggest a long and fruitful interaction with humankind. They are mentioned in treatises going back centuries. As such they are eternal, in the sense that an individual is all individuals of the same species. This is where he is in his understanding, at least. So how do you approach a being that is timeless? In his case, you didn't. You couldn't. A gap was waiting to be bridged.

Most of his visitors know basic things about most Mediterranean plants though. They are no strangers to woofing. Some count botany as one of their personal interests. Those asked questions, and he was proud when his theoretical learning allowed him to answer. They started to harvest leaves, cut off buds or flowers, unearth roots, and then dry, chop, macerate, concoct and infuse, reduce to powder, burn and extract pigment. He just followed along. All the movements were simple, he simply had to imitate them- what is more tricky is the logic underlying them. He does as they do, and reaps the same fruits.

They find themselves in the garden for hours, covering humid soil with ewe dung, planting rows of baby plants, or potatoes or cabbages, harvesting fava beans or green peas. All these names of boring plants he was forced to ingest as a child in the era of supermarkets actually correspond, he now realizes, to plants, with their own behaviour and aspect. Also, they are a miracle and a delight, when before they were just healthy food. It isn't the same when you go to the plant, pick what you need, walk back home, and cook it. He knows his sense of wonderment is ridiculous, and it betrays him as what he sadly is: an ignorant city-dweller. He can't help it though. The contrast is too impressive.

THE GREAT ALIVENESS OF THINGS

Life points up, mostly, but also hangs down, flows horizontally, burrows, and undulates. Generally, plants look for the sun, and mobile beasts feed on them and then on each other. Some sex-ed principles can be guessed at there; everyone is trying to eat each other or fuck each other, and sometimes both at the same time. Great interspecies sex parties are organized involving ivy, bees and the wind, or figs and wasps, or dolphins and dead fish, or so he's heard. Everybody is itching at the crotch, everybody needs nutrients to go through their ever filling, ever emptying bellies. Dead things become the living materials they are made out of; fungi do their mysterious things in hidden places, glowing with satisfaction, holding keys to the mysteries of life. Whenever you stick your head outside, wasps and hornets come investigate you, flies eat your skin and drink the sweat from it, and you look down and a band of wild pigs has been going at the grapes and figs in your garden all night. A few steps toward the river, and there you find the bloodstained feathers of some bird, who was probably also feeding on the grapes when a weasel caught it and bled it. Birds fly away at your step, convinced of your harmfulness; you are of the same kind, to them, as the weasels, wildcats and foxes, or as the hawks who hunt them from the sky.

BIRDWATCHING

It is May, and birds come and go that are visible from the terrace, where most shared time is spent, on the long wooden table it was made to accommodate. Long breakfasts, short lunches, long dinners are all taken here, under the teardrop light above which a hog's jaw has been hung by someone a long time ago, before all this. In between meals, people prepare them here, and also prepare a multitude of other things, plant medicine, small sculptures, paint that is made from things in the garden or one of the two hills, etcetera. People draw, read, write emails, and potter about in various ways, alone or in groups, but mostly in groups because there is always someone here, and in consequence, this is where you come when you're feeling social.

Birdwatching is done alone or in small groups, and the point, I think, is to silently sit or lie down in a strategic position to see a specific species of birds. One imagines birdwatchers as people dressed in tactical gear, lying down in a bush, with a pair of binoculars close at hand and a small notepad to write down observations and maybe even sketch whatever you're observing. So one would think that the most social place in the area would essentially be the worst for watching birds. And yet, there is a hoopoe nesting in the wall above the outside stairs, a pair of starlings in a hole in one of the huge plane trees that border the terrace, a robin that is always flitting about around the bamboo grove, hated gangs of jackdaws that come spread their aura of danger near the river, and then tits, sparrows, ravens and goldfinches that come visit, and then the eagle-owl, the tawny owl, and armies of bats that come alive as night falls. The starlings are of a source of endless mirth, as they paranoically fly from branch to branch with huge bugs or cherries in their beaks before flying down to their nest to feed them to their babies, in a deluded attempt to trump a potential predator's vigilance. Being predators themselves, in a sense, they can attest to how deluded that is. The Hoopoe is an exotic wonder that raises cries of delight whenever its strange butterfly-like flight and extravagant plumage is spotted, going from one end of the garden to the other, perching on high branches and thinking of who-knows-what. What is interesting with animals is to attempt empathy, and then read up and find out the limits to the possibility of such, like night vision, an excellent sense of smell, or worse: flight. Or living your life in water. Just imagining is a pleasing game though, and it is a recurring feature of time spent at the long table on the terrace. Then, when animals become eerily more present, both physically and through the traces they leave, more vivid and alive, in a word: more relatable, it becomes apparent that their pleasant game had deeper implications for how you live in the world.

STRENGTH IS SEXY

The contingent is happier naked. Now the sun shines everyday and the temperatures are pleasant, bare skin is ubiquitous and skin becomes exposed. Everyday, most bathe naked in the river, or with just underwear or just a piece of cloth around their privates. They lie down in the sun and let it dry their skin; they roll around in the dirt and then go wash it away. Heat allows for civilization to dissolve more easily- you only need food and water and a good blanket at night, and thoughts, no longer made uneasy by the permanent discomfort of wind or weather, become lighter. They all delight in feeling primitive, though no one says the word or anything resembling it; it is a given and a tacit understanding. People will be lauded and joined by involved comrades if they start squatting, half naked, their feet in the ash left from yesterday's fire, nibbling at meat from a bone. Food needs little preparation, and bodies don't need as much of it; everyone can feel lighter when the sun heats the world up. Sounds become more vibrant, and odours too. When walking through the garden, you are hit with clouds of rosemary, Damascus roses, thyme, wormwood, rue, water mint and all the rest; at times the earth itself smells like honey. The sweat from their bodies evokes hops, marijuana or overripe fruits; the river has a green, muddy smell that stays on the body even after you dry. Fires leave fiery smells, green and tangy or deep and brown. Heat wraps bodies in pleasant bubbles, and coming in and out of the houses becomes an experience in itself, because its thick walls and strategically placed windows and corridors keep it cool and gloomy: you come into the kitchen to eat a strawberry from the huge pile that was picked yesterday afternoon, and overpowering chills travel up your naked back, ending in discreet ecstasy at the back of your skull. Then you come out again, and the heat catches you whole like the all-embracing arms of some fertile god.

He likes to take a break, while weeding, for example, and observe the muscles, hairs and eyes of his friends as they continue. They are alive; very alive; just as alive as the bird that is carefully looking for worms right there, or the mysterious lizard, perfectly immobile and the hot metal of an abandoned truck at the corner of the field. He can see the concept of labour illustrated, visible at last: human beings are moving their limbs and intelligences in a coordinated fashion, and producing results that maintain and augment their livelihood.

JUDITH AS FERTILITY

Her body emerges from a pond, revealed by diffuse light, its form the result of a chopping away at raw stone. The matrix was an egg, and the egg revealed this heavy archaic form, the bust of a woman, Judith the statue, cut from its legs at the top of its thighs, just beneath the pubic area. There is a slight smile on the lips, and the eyes are glasses where light swirls like yellow wine. There are greenish reflections and transparencies where angles catch the light, but the skin is moving, breathing somehow. All around are tall dark trees; they bend towards her figure. Blades of grass, leaves and flowers are pointing toward her, like so many hands trying to grasp. Everything points upward.

He wakes up; his mind is eerily lucid. After a while, he starts to wonder whether this is going too far.

IS THIS UTOPIA?

It is impossible to mistake this for anything else: this is a period of bliss. When they have dinner all together, ten different preparations are put on the table, with ingredients that are obscenely fresh, which for the most part grew from the very soil their chairs are rested on, and the rest from well-liked neighbours that are known by name, whose family you talk about as you eat the meat from their sheep, their green chard with eggs, or cheese from their goats. Sometimes you even know the goats by name. Wine is poured that evokes precious stones both in aspect and, with only a slight stretch, taste; candles are lit that make everyone more handsome and mysterious, make them emerge from the warm obscurity like bodies in a Georges de la Tour painting. Three languages are permanently being mixed, forming elegant hybrids, and it is not rare, four hours after the meal, to find most of the group still talking, murmuring just above the rustling of the leaves and cries of night-birds, or howling with laughter.

As in an ideal F. Scott Fitzgerald party, the table frequently starts hovering four feet above the ground.

Life is thick, healthy, juicy, with all the tastes and textures their bodies have, that the food they eat has. Everyone is well-fed, well-rested, well-sexed and sweet-smelling. They rub themselves with kaolin to make their skin soft. They massage each other with oils infused with powerful smells. They paint their faces and bodies, and mix found clothes and created ones to become fantastic creatures. They dance.

Their life is almost obscenely luxurious, in fact, and the Spanish contingent is not a group to forget the various flavours of misery that pervade most spaces outside of this valley.

References are made to mass migration, Capitalism, Liberalism, Colonialism, the Patriarchy, Empire; these spectres hang above their heads, ominous and grave, inescapably present. They are only escaping them by chance, they know, and only for a while. Maybe even through sheer helplessness or worse: cowardice. Some aren't far from thinking that. Though they are outcasts and bridge-burners, the lot of them, many paths connect them still to abstractions whose existence they disapprove of, but nonetheless participate in: governments, police and military forces and banks, mostly, and everything that derives from them, but also more tenuous, less defined abstractions, ideas that float around in culture: progress, respectability, a career, setting something aside for your old days, and then also success, beauty, glamour, happiness, love, and their negative mirrors: failure, misery, squalor, madness, depression, loneliness. Oh, they all have a good idea which perspectives are more fruitful concerning these spectres, and yet, they are inhabited by them, right down to the invisible parts of themselves.

The perspective from which they consider and condemn things as traps, lies and agendas is a miracle of the intellect, and belongs to that realm. There is a rift between the relative positions of the moral concepts they use to map the world, in the intellectual realm, and their effective distance in their life. Good and bad when you daydream are two enemies fighting, or a great dragon on one side and a brave shepherd on the other, but in practise they use the same canals, proceed from similar causes, and co-exist within them and their groups. They know this, and hence, they also know they will go back into the world, back to work, back to fighting losing battles. Like heroic battles in movies, there is no other way, and unlike them, there is no show, and no public: everyone is both.

But also intimacy and fluid acceptance, because it must be so: though outliers within it, they belong to their culture; they reap part of its bounties and share in the pains that come with them.

Most of them share a dream, of one day settling their group defined by speed, energy and nomadism, precisely in a place like this, and build something with all the skills they have acquired during their travels. For some reason, though, and somehow they all know: now is not the time for that, and this is not the place for it. Maybe they aren't ready for utopia. Besides, none of them thinks that's what they'll be aiming for, when they do settle. You need money to live, they are all aware, and till they don't need it anymore, it won't be utopia.

JUDITH AS AN ANTIQUARIAN

In this dream, Judith is the owner of an antique shop and he is a potential buyer. Their meeting is not fortuitous, he knows; there have been long exchanges of emails leading up to this. He is looking for something very specific and rare, and she has claimed that she has it. She is showing him some etchings, and then some eglomisé glass images. At one point she hands him a small sous verre painting whose colours, with a red dominant, are eye-catching. It is him in the drawing, in the style of an 18th century fantasy; he is a red being or dressed in a kind of red pajama. His head is horned, and his eyes are on either side of his skull. He is giving a lecture to a multitude of humanoid characters, drawn in shades of blue, who are sitting on the ground around him. He realizes he is the devil, and this is Sabbath, and the priests are after him and want to throw him in the ground in a heavy lead sarcophagus. An urgent sense of having to flee comes over him, and he screams and tries to run, but his legs have already been cut off or turned to lead. Judith the antiquarian has stopped moving, like a robot with a malfunction.

Then he wakes up in his warm bed, wrapped in wonderful old rough sheets, a sweet light coming in through the window. Valentine is by his side, still sleeping, with the innocent look that sleep gives to faces. He snuggles up to her and listens to the birds chirping, calm and satisfied.

A RESURGENCE (SELF DECEIT?)

Things are always shifting. There is no way around it. The secret, everyone knows at some point (before forgetting again), is to shift along with things; no one is able to do it though. If they were, they would be saints.

He was walking in the garden, noticing things as he is now wont to do, and looking for a place where to sit, from which he might notice things unfolding in time. What a blissful project. It has been his ambition for a day or two now, but he has held off attempting it, for fear of rushing things. He finally finds a clearing amongst the grasses, just large enough to fit his arse and folded legs. There are probably some ants there, he knows from the small holes in the hard, dry ground, but he chooses not to care.

He sits, and looks in front of him, focussing on nothing in particular. From the ground up, it is verticality that dominates, criss-crossed by a chaos of branches, leaves, vines, and in the background, the yellow humid sandstone above the riverbank. There are directions: the garden, river and wind from north-west to south-east, or from left to right, the sun from south-west to north-east, or from behind to in front of him, piercing down into the river, calm and transparent, lively but calm, where red and green stones create ripples and subtle currents.

He notices a continuity between himself, his living breathing body, insects buzzing about, plants rustling and waving, the river flowing, the wind blowing, and the elated cries of Esme, Jorge and Miguel further up the river (they are trying to fish with a harpoon they made). What is this continuity? It manifests through the continuous unfolding of now, the renewal of nowness, to the beat of his breath. It is too much information to process in any way but one, and that way is, to say the least, mysterious. He tries it, though; you never know, and that is, he thinks, what his ambition was.

Suddenly, as he tries to experience the continuity between phenomena, a chill travels up his spine, followed by heat in his whole body, and a feeling of stillness. Not stiffness, but irreversible solidity. His brain is still registering all of the stimuli, and as such there is movement, and he is breathing. But all activity from within himself has ceased. The power that creates the stillness is inside his body, but it is also all around. All the information he perceives seems to emanate from it. This lasts for a few minutes, maybe, and then his body gives in. He doesn't change position, or at least not perceptibly, but the stillness has left him. What he feels now is hollowness, and then joy; joy so thick it is like sadness or pain. It makes him cry. He is positively bawling. His body shakes with emotion. Then the thick joy recedes, and he is left panting, his eyes still wet, wondering what the hell just happened- slightly worried. He needs to pee, and when he gets up to go do so in the river, his knees and legs are sore from sitting for so long. His cranium is like an empty pierced coconut, which the sun shines through.

JUDITH AS THE SUN

In this dream, he is lying on the ground, facing the sky. Stuck to the ground, in fact. He somehow knows that the ground is his grandfather (his actual father's father, a man he admires in waking life without knowing very much about him) who in the dream is also a dragon; and the sky is permeated with bright light. The bright light is Judith, and in the centre of it is the sun, which is also Judith. He has the sense that she is speaking to his body. He is utterly stuck to the ground; if he wanted to get up, he couldn't. The force keeping him down is overpowering, so powerful that it has the potential to derail his mind entirely if he doesn't somehow digest it. It is a superfood, he thinks at some point, terrified.

Waves of disgustingly nutritious light are undulating throughout his body. They start at the back of his head, pass behind his closed lips, go through his chest like a bubble of hot air, then through the stomach like food, enter beneath the pubic bone, and then diffuse through the legs. Every wave is accompanied with a corresponding movement of the whole body, as though to help it go through. It is an endless loop of muscle contractions, designed to keep the odious light flowing. If it stops, his mind will shatter in the most disgusting, alien, irreversible way, he knows it, so he must keep the loop going : a contraction of the forehead, pursing of the lips, swallowing, breathing in, contraction of the abdominal muscles, lifting of the hips, a shiver, and then it goes back to the top. Judith, the Sun, isn't communicating in any other way than permeating the whole dome of the sky with awful, inescapable, weird and inhuman bright light. It is so nutritious it could kill him. There is only the vast dome of the sky, weird and alien, and the vast dome of the ground on which he lays, reassuring and strong. He is in the middle, trying not to lose it.

When he wakes up from this, his body is still undulating. He gasps for air, feeling as though he just escaped a terrifying danger. He lays there, doing nothing but looking up at the ceiling, for far too long. His thoughts are a muddled mess. He perceives the smells from the garden as acidic, pungent, heavy, and somehow in the know, more so than he is, about what just happened to him.

THE BOOK AGAIN

Jorge and Maribel are bunking together these days, and they have elected to do so in what was Esme and Maribel's room till then; which happens to be the room where he found refuge on the night he was terrified by the dry hairiness of the ground, and then found the strange book.

Presently, he is lounging on the bed with just Jorge, who is writing in his notebook. He is doing nothing much, mostly trying to refrain from noticing too many things, for fear he might become a stone and then start crying again. His body is sensitive though, to every stimulus available, which is physically pleasing and frightening to his sense of masculinity at the same time. What kind of man are you if the texture of the blanket makes the hair on your forearms stand on end, and the way an old plastered wall catches the light makes your anus twitch, he feels, responding to the low, grunting whispers of his unenlightened forebears. Surely it is simpler to just hide a well of repressed emotion within yourself, and play along with whatever being a man means to most men. Then again, if he chose that path (again), he would no longer be eligible to the friendship of the contingent, who he has chosen for his teachers and leaders of the way. Still, he wishes he weren't so permeable to everything happening. This is what happens when you start noticing everything.

It is also quite nice, he thinks, in the sense that something is really happening. It is somewhat akin to what happens in superhero origin stories, though more vague of course, because no spider bit him, and no mad scientist experimented on his body. He was visited by a ghost, and then all of this happened. Still, something in his perception of reality has markedly changed, perhaps for the better; perhaps he is going crazy, too, but as long as he is locked in his madness, he might as well explore the frankly more interesting world that madness has opened up for him. That being settled, he turns to the bookshelf by the bed, not thinking of the strange book he found there months ago, and starts reading the titles on the spines. When he finds the book again and opens it, the central red drawing reappears. The person in the boat is staring, maybe inviting him in, maybe judging him, or maybe looking right through him and at something that is part of the drawings' world, but not drawn. He looks at it for a while, fascinated by the turn of events, and then puts it back on the shelf again.

JUDITH REAPPEARS

Her teeth are as strong as ever. She smiles as she exits the car and hugs him, and then smiles less and less as they pass to the terrace, where Tiny and Maribel are grinding down some stone without any restraint or order to make pigment (Maribel has decorated her face and shoulders with the red powder- Pedrito is naked, and his sticky skin has taken on a demonic hue) entered the kitchen to get coffee, exit the kitchen where the big table was covered in dried animal skull-bones that Jorge has been drying to build a macabre chandelier from, and walk out to the table in the garden. Jorge is squatting in the ashes of yesterday's fire, looking for a piece of clay he had lodged inside a log to see whether it would harden. He is wearing a loincloth, and looks like a performance artist working on the theme of animality. Judith's lips purse slightly. He looks at her proudly. For some reason, Judith then spends her whole visit telling him about her hippie days living on communes, trying to find authenticity. The message is clear: I have tried this, too, and it leads nowhere. He tells her about the ghost. Her lips purse extremely, and then recede to form a satisfied, powerful, predatory smile. It blinds him like the sun. As he accompanies her back to her car and she's about to get behind the wheel to drive off, she suddenly hugs him. It's the first time she does that. Her arms are strong; her body feels hard. She whispers: "maybe you should go back to the city". He doesn't answer, but hugs her back with vulnerable intensity.

DRAMA

It came suddenly, just as the tide turns, though when reflecting back they would see the process had started weeks before. Jorge started to walk around alone more, humming to himself, and spent most of the rest of his time alone in a room. He talked about a show they were about to start preparing, back in Berlin where he had studied- him and Esme have been invited to participate. Was it as a result of that, or just a coincidence? The others became more restless, and started to plan more, and make projects for the future. Joanna wanted to go to Sevilla to learn about tinctorial plants with a woman she knew there. Tiny and Thaïs were planning their trip to a collective farm- Thaïs knew the founder. Miguel was tagging along; he wanted to learn more about vernacular architectural techniques. The contingent was about to move along- it was in the air.

Where a cult-like serenity had pervaded the air, small disagreements started erupting. One night Maribel and Joanna started piling friendly criticism on Esme, who left crying. The following day, Jorge (ever Esme's ally) threw rough shade at Joanna concerning her appearance. She didn't leave crying: she yelled at him, and he yelled back. Miguel started hitting on Valentine a lot more heavily, and she responded by calling him a pig. Our hero was thinking of Judith and what she had told him.

DISSOLUTION

After the drama started erupting, everything went very fast. Esme and Jorge packed their bags and asked him to take them to the bus station. They had a train leaving from Montpellier four hours from now. It was morning still, and it was one of those days when you never quite wake up. Something of the stickiness of sleep stays in your face and eyes. There were strong winds, and small clouds travelled fast, making the sun flicker on and off again. At the station they all hugged and promised they would see each other again soon. No one thought to imagine when that would be. He felt like a hypocrite, being certain that if he did see any of them again, it wouldn't be soon. He drove back home slowly, smoking cigarettes through the car's open window, first thinking of strictly nothing but the road, and then wondering. Thinking of himself as a character in a story, he tried to analyse his arc and what bothered him about it. We expect stories to take us somewhere, he reflected- somewhere like a destination. A house surrounded by trees and a garden to build fires in- that was a destination. He should've arrived, according to his own analysis, and then the story would have ended. But it now appeared as though the house, the garden and the fires had simply been another event, another vicissitude, leading up to more stuff in the straight line of time, itself a linear journey from birth to death. It seemed to him for a while that his understanding of stories and time was a morbid one. Maybe there was a flicker of knowing, at this time (like feeling a shard under skin again, but still separated from his touch), of what time and stories actually felt like. Then he arrived at the house.

Four days later, Pedrito said he was leaving tomorrow. Maribel, Miguel and Thaïs stayed a few more days.

TRAIN AGAIN

A call came the previous day from his father, from whom he hadn't heard in a while. He thought this might be him fishing for news from his son, trying to figure out what is going on in his new life, if he's happy and thriving or hiding in despair. If he has money, or no money. The thought that he was being checked on by the patriarch reassured him for a second, and he remembered how large and strong his father's hand felt around his when he was a child. Instead, though, he was unceremoniously beckoned back to Paris as fast as possible. The phone call was unpleasant: there was a lingering feeling of reproach from his father at his absence from all of the collective family turbulences leading up to this last hospitalization.

It's true, he was hardly aware his grandfather had been dying. He had spoken to no member of his family, preferring to forget temporarily that he had been born attached to this group of people, his family, and focus instead on a new group with whom he was learning new things, the contingent. One doesn't escape the tethers of love and pain and shared habit that have been wrought for years by caring parents, when they, as his have, have invested so much in creating and then strengthening the bonds of that apparently most sacred matrix, the nuclear family, to the extent that all of the people they have most loved or at least, frequented, also become the foreground of their children's life. Having no good reason to break the bonds brutally, you don't break them at all; you remain attached to a seemingly randomly chosen group of people, whom you've known and who have known you your whole life. That's just the way it is, and it is good for that reason. He is in that situation. Just like a plant grows wherever its seed has happened to arrive into favourable soil, this is where it will live out its existence. He must go and witness his grandfather's departure, and bond again with his first and most enduring tribe in the most bond-forming circumstance: death.

As the train moves fast through landscapes that have been cut open for it by human ingenuity, he looks out the window as he always does, neglecting to take notice of any of his surroundings except for his neighbour, Valentine, the only token of life he has left. He loves her. How easy it is to forget. The hills, trees and pastures give way to high moats that hide everything. The moat plunges back into the ground, and there is a forest. A wide sky above flat land becomes a tunnel. A tunnel opens up on a wall; the wall disappears into a beautiful farmhouse, far too close to the tracks. Hills become plains. Plains become wide expanses of industrial architecture. A water treatment facility, several cheap hotels, a parking lot. Then houses and blocks of buildings. Several empty stations pass by fast, the blue signs on which their names are inscribed rendered illegible by speed. Then the tracks become deeper, seemingly gouged into the ground, and around are high old walls, covered in graffiti. They are back in the city. He is back in Paris.

DEATH

Is it sad? It should be sad; he loved his grandpa. He was so worn out from Alzheimer's and old age though, there wasn't much really left of him. This is what our victorious times do to death, he thinks. It comes as liberation from a world that desperately wants to keep you alive, because your life is valuable and sacred, perhaps for no other reason than because it is important to those around you. By the time you die, though, that life has become a frightening shadow, an abstraction almost, more discernible from the movements on the ECG than from your demeanour or certainly your lifestyle which becomes that of a cadaver. Sometimes you open your eyes though, and a sickly look attests to your clinical aliveness. Does something remain from the person you once were? Affection, certainly, and the longing for it. You cling to the hands of your bedside visitors, and sometimes you shed a tear. People talk, trying to read your minimal reactions. You hear what they are saying, but your body is becoming less animate, more heavy, all the while your mind is becoming lighter, fainter, more desynchronized from this realm. Your eyes become veiled with a certain opaqueness. Then one day, you die, and people say "he suffered so much, it was time for him to go". "It's better that way". Maybe it is. The taste of the end is sour; its rhythm is slow. Then there are ceremonies for the living, and the dead are left behind in confusion.

He arrives in the hospital a little too late- his grandfather did not wait for him. His lifeless body is lying on the bed, perfectly symmetrical. The body is very obviously lifeless, drained of life- whatever that is. It is deflated. An object. He has been asked if he wanted to be alone with it for a while, and has said yes. He contemplates what was the face of his father's father, and has no thoughts, feels no emotion. His eyes see yellowy, waxy skin, loosely wrapped around sharp bones. A hyperrealistic mask. There are brown marks, a redness around one eye, a few hairs popping out of unexpected places. He touches his grandfather's cold hand. It is limp. He is as dead as a dead wild hog, a dead sparrow, a dead lizard. More dead than a dried plant. Less dead than a dead stone. As dead as a rotten onion. More dead than a flowing river. As dead as a good painting; less dead than a bad one.

This game of comparisons is pointless. He leaves the room and rejoins his weeping aunt, whom he hugs. Valentine is here, wearing a sad, restrained face he is sure isn't fabricated, but utterly sincere. They are going to his father's house today; the mass and burial is tomorrow.

BURIAL

On an adequately overcast day, a black-clad party of family and friends walks from the church to the cemetery with the coffin containing his grandfather's dead body. Everyone is visibly stricken with sadness, as silent and unmoving as they can be; the only sounds that arise among the timid cries of birds and the priests' soliloquy are some discreet sobs, some noses being blown, a baby's cry, instantly muffled and brought a little way away from the sad group. Flowers are thrown on the glossy wood, along with pieces of paper bearing last words that couldn't be said out loud. Then some symbolic earth is thrown on top, before the actual burial, which will be left to an unconcerned worker equipped with obscenely professional tools after the party's departure. He is waiting by the side with his yellow excavator. His grey, weathered shirt and relaxed posture indicate that he's not including himself in the ritual. Just doing his job.

He maintains a composure in line with the others; most around here are older than him, so they must know what to do under such circumstances. He feels hollow, acting out his part; and yet not filled by it. If he were filled by it, or filling it, his thoughts would also be in line with his posture and the rhythm of his movements. Instead, they are dancing around the most superficial details, and latching onto them firmly before flitting away. The priest's face is rugged; his hands look like an agricultor's hands. The ribbon on this woman's hat is coming off. It's funny how big feet can be compared to a person's size. Babies really always do their own thing; if they were adults, they would be considered autistic. My grandfather's body is in the box. Valentine is crying discreetly, how pretty she is when she cries. It's interesting, the type of sadness we are performing; complicated, really. You must be sad, but sad in accordance to your status in the hierarchy of grieving. If you cry too hard or for too long, but aren't considered a member of the departed's closest circle, you may be seen as a faker, or as trying to steal the shine of those whose sadness is justified by structure and established knowledge. On the other hand, if, say, you are a member of that circle, and your demeanour is closer to that of a bouncer than a virgin Mary in despair, meaning you are performing the coldness of death without the emotions of grieving, you may be seen as empty or deluded, or inhuman. If you're simply an acquaintance, you could be suspected of just being here for the networking value of the event, or maybe even just for the free wine. This one is going well though; peoples' performances are convincing and harmonious; if erring a little on the side of coldness rather than emotion. Mom's eyes have not moved in a while now, they must be dried out. Dad is a mirror, I think his facial muscles are all paralysed. He is repressing like hell, I'm sure. That priest has got to be capable of lifting up a wrecked car without any help to save a crushed puppy underneath. I wonder what you think at the moment of dying? It must be a surprising sensation. A powerful one. I need coffee. Like being wrenched out of your body perhaps. Or maybe like a surge from within; like a death wave arising from the belly. Or from the heart. Maybe you feel your heart slowing down, and the feeling is one of slowing down; or maybe it accelerates, and the feeling is one of acceleration. Of being launched. Of taking off. Like on a plane when you are not yet used to planes, and as the plane accelerates for the take-off, you think: "is this take-off? Is this it?" every accelerating second, and the feeling of acceleration augments in ways that you hadn't thought were possible, and yet you still think "Is it now? It must be now", and it still accelerates, and you aren't sure whether you're in the air or not, but then when the plane actually rises above the ground, you know it truly, without any doubt, because you can feel a distinct break between the hard, straight, exerting feeling of the wheels on the tarmac, their friction, and the sudden feeling of floating, of gliding, of not being in contact with anything but air. And then you keep flying off and the actual journey starts.

SAMENESS ON THE SIDEWALK

A small and discreet cocktail party has been organized at a bar just outside the cemetery; everybody's here, or almost. The thing is done. Adequate roles have been played out. Bodies have been bound in stillness and silence, minds have called to the idea of death in general, and of this death in particular; they have bidden farewell, both with measured non-committal movements for the outside world, and with heartfelt, genuine words within themselves, to the departed old man. A shared feeling of having done something correctly is usually the guarantee of a good party; most feel relatively freed from the pressure to perform sadness and are now content to drink wine and chat. It is a pleasant moment, where anecdotes are shared, and laughing is permitted again, though in most immediately followed by a restraining of it, out of a sense of not knowing where decency imposes you to moderate your mirth. His father laughs, though, because he is allowed to lead the path for the rest, emotionally, being the closest to the departed as his only son, and the new patriarch. So others laugh, too, and the atmosphere is joyful. This will be remembered as one of those paradoxically joyful funerals, where everything went well and the memory of the dead one was celebrated not only in pain, but also in joy. Everyone wants that for themselves.

Valentine leaves at one point, having a previous engagement that she has delayed attending because of the occasion's momentum. He accompanies her outside, and for a while they kiss and hug, and speak lightly. He thanks her for being there. She wouldn't have dreamt of not coming. It is simply natural. This is quite unlike how he still left when her great-uncle died, at the beginning of the story, leaving her alone to deal with it, he reflects out loud, not quite apologizing but acknowledging the gap in class between their respective courses of action under similar circumstances. She says yes. Some part of him was hoping to be reassured, to be told, perhaps, that he did well to follow his instinct, and look, it lead us back here, happier and enriched and standing stronger on the ground, etc. He would like to find a good, sellable backstory (mostly just for himself, at least for a start) for how he met his ghost. She doesn't provide it, though- and she won't. It feels more like he has left the rhythm for a while. No comment is made about that. Life can be easy and good now, perhaps. He walks with her to where the metro station is, and they joke a little and then they kiss in a way that feels nice, and she leaves.

Walking back to the bar, he goes back in his mind to this sensation of having left the rhythm, or of being accused of that. His return to it (through this ceremony of burial, and his return to Paris) makes it all the more apparent. He's back. He won't resist. It's just as when he left Paris for the south: after all, why not? There would be a thousand things to do with the contingent, or that kind of crowd if not them, things that seem like the best a person can do in this world. But they are not for him. They demand a break from a previous state of affairs. Otherwise, everything brings him back to where he is from. There isn't enough momentum, be it in himself or outside, if such a thing as outside exists, to take him out of the path he's on.

Whatever that is. He isn't disgusted enough by the way his previous life was, perhaps. Maybe not deluded enough for utopia. Maybe his ghost isn't strong enough. He is, he reflects, one of the most normal, unadventurous, tepid people he knows.

As he crosses the street, a scooter passes by neither fast nor slowly, neither noisily nor silently. He doesn't see the rider's face, but as the scooter speeds away, he feels as though it is hauling an enormous net, and in the net, far away down the street, is a huge black void, eating at the city. He gets to the other side, unbothered, and a wind follows in the same direction. The top of his mind is blown away by it. It appears that there is nothing underneath, nothing but perhaps a faint glow. His mouth is agape for a moment; he's still walking, avoiding passers-by and everything, and also he is like a bowl where the wind is swirling. It is neither warm nor cold. It has no texture or character. It shines perhaps a little. There is nothing else.

THE END

Milton Keynes UK
Ingram Content Group UK Ltd.
UKHW010841190424
441445UK00001B/47